Ludwig Thoma's Rascal Stories

Philipp Strazny

Für meine Eltern,
die solche Sachen immer
im Regal stehen hatten

Contents

Translator's Foreword.. 7

Chapter 1: The Elegant Boy.. 16

Chapter 2: Summer Vacations... 33

Chapter 3: Mydears 48

Chapter 4: Good Resolutions.. 67

Chapter 5: Betterment.. 79

Chapter 6: Uncle Franz 94

Chapter 7: Perjury.. 100

Chapter 8: The Engagement 109

Chapter 9: Gretchen Vollbeck.. 117

Chapter 10: The Wedding 127

Chapter 11: My First Love 140

Chapter 12: The Baby 150

About the Author 160

About the Translator 161

TRANSLATOR'S FOREWORD

Ludwig Thoma published his *Rascal Stories* in 1905. If I remember correctly, my great-grandmother read this book as a child - she was born in 1904. My grandmother read it, and my mother did as well. This is significant, because this part of my family inhabited Silesia at the beginning of the 20th century. Thus, even "Prussian" children enjoyed Thoma's writing, even though he decidedly wrote as a Bavarian, and Bavarians have always been anti-Prussian, and in some ways they still are, at least jokingly. Given that I grew up north of Frankfurt, I was myself just another "Prussian" child who giggled reading about Ludwig's shenanigans.

If you search for information on Thoma today, you will frequently find mention that he is revered as a Bavarian author, as if he had only geographically limited appeal. However, besides the national reach of his books, the *Rascal Stories* were turned into a successful movie in the 1960s, followed by six other "franchise" movies before interest finally waned.

It is possible that both the enduring success with children as well as the success at the office box made the book suspect as literature. In Germany, popular appeal was and is often not regarded as compatible with artistic quality. A further damning aspect was the fact that Thoma penned a number of anti-Semitic rants near the end of his life. Given that post-war literary critics generally assumed an anti-fascist stance, they likely preferred to take a pass on praising even the early work of a clearly tainted author.

Rereading the novel as an adult is a curious experience. It does contain many funny scenes, and many clearly go over a child's head. I suspect,

for example, that a child reader would gloss over the allusions to alcohol and its effects. Furthermore, an adult reader may be more at liberty to take an outside perspective, while a child would be caught in that of the I-narrator. Both perspectives certainly have their appeal, and it may be debatable which one is funnier.

The main character, Ludwig, is obviously a troublemaker, a nightmare for teachers and relatives. Although we experience his world from his perspective, an adult reader may at times be torn between sympathy, pity, and outright dislike. Growing up fatherless, Ludwig is yearning for affirmation from an adult man, and whenever he feels rejected, he lashes out. He turns violent against persons weaker than him: he does not hesitate to slap a girl at school to "put her in her place", and he engages in animal torture to get at the owners. Today's teachers would not only wonder whether he might become a political anarchist, but they might worry about having a budding sociopath on their hands.

That said, despite a couple of instances where the reader's laughter stops in remorse, the content of Thoma's memories is a far cry from aberrations depicted in today's novels, and the book is definitely entertaining. Furthermore, the humor arising from people treating each other roughly was popular at the time, as evidenced by the cartoons of Wilhelm Busch - a fellow contributor to the satirical *Simplicissimus* weekly. As all Germans know, *Schadenfreude ist die schönste Freude* (seeing others in trouble is the greatest fun).

While the *Rascal Stories* pretend to be autobiographical, and they undoubtedly are as far as the general setting is concerned, they are clearly fictionalized, with neat psychological explanations (Ludwig's search for a father figure), relatively logical chronology, fitting dialog, and a narrator who is able to remember minutest details. Anybody who has ever told and retold a funny occurrence knows how stories take on a life of their own, gaining embellishments for dramatic effect. Whether any of these things actually happened to Thoma or his classmates is unknowable at this point and wholly irrelevant.

The geographical references in the story are not terribly helpful in pinning down the exact location. Thoma spent at least some time at school in *Burghausen*, while his mother ran a tavern in *Prien am Chiemsee*. Neither of these places are mentioned by name, but *Mühlhausen* is mentioned several times. In Chapter 3, the Holy Aloysius arrives by rack wagon from *Mühlhausen*. *Mühlhausen* also has a train

Burghausen an der Donau, Google Maps

station that is reachable by "mail omnibus" (i.e. a horse-drawn carriage for multiple passengers). Furthermore, the train from *Mühlhausen* stops in *Endorf* on the way

Prien am Chiemsee, Google Maps

home. Thus, it is likely that most of the school scenes take place in *Burghausen*, while "home" is located in *Prien am Chiemsee*:

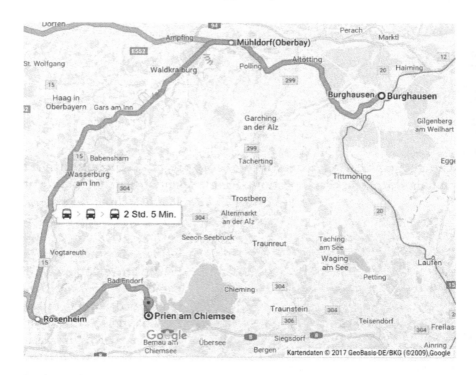

Burghausen is ca. 30 km (20 m) from Mühlhausen, for which Google estimates 2 hours by bicycle, so this was certainly doable by horse carriage. "Uncle Franz", however, lives in a larger city, which may be either Landstuhl or Landshut, two of the other stations in Thoma's tortuous school career. However, while Thoma makes sufficient references to roughly place the story in southern Bavaria, he also omits enough information to keep it in literary no-man's land.

During the translation, I found myself stuck in several places, wondering whether I should "correct" stylistic errors in the source text. There is repetitive wording. There are run-on sentences. In some cases, it is not immediately clear who a pronoun refers to. In other cases, the tense is off, and the text jumps from past tense to present and back. It may very well be that this "poor writing" kept the book from being regarded as good literature.

However, I have come to believe that Thoma used bad style deliberately, and that he carefully crafted this style in order to "stay in character." In the first story, we are told that Ludwig goes to "first

grade of Latin school", which would be the first grade of post-elementary school or fifth grade in modern counting. By chapter nine, he would be in eighth grade, and at the end of the book, his sister returns home with a small toddler, so Ludwig would be in tenth or eleventh grade.

As Ludwig gets older, the narrator's style also matures. Where the first chapter uses simple vocabulary for purely chronological telling of events ("and then..., and then..., and then..."), the language in later chapters measurably increases in complexity.

If we take words like "and, but, then, there" as markers of juvenile language, we see a steady drop in their frequency per chapter (indicated by the trend line):

Juvenile Wording

Frequencies of Und, Dann, Da, Aber per total words in chapter

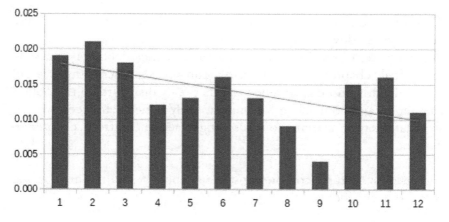

Inversely, we see an increase in sentence length:

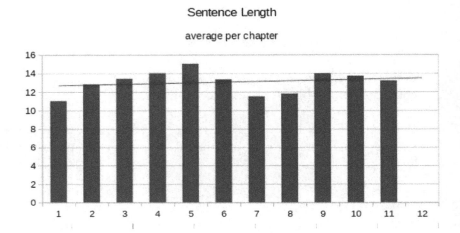

Note that I did not include the last chapter here, because the "baby talk" drives down its average sentence length to 8.8 words. Furthermore, I used "and" and "but" as sentence delimiters, because the initial chapters contain many run-on sentences that would artificially drive up the sentence length. So, by disregarding the outlier chapter 12 and controlling for unnecessarily joined sentences, we can see that there is a trend towards longer sentences from chapter to chapter.

Alongside structural complexity, the vocabulary also matures as the protagonist gets older:

Unique Words

Proportion of Total Words in Chapter

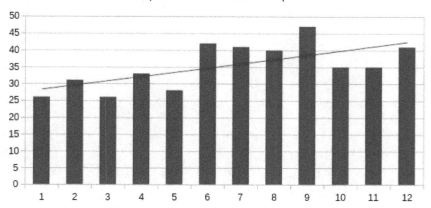

While initial chapters are told with limited, repetitive vocabulary, later chapters employ a larger variety of words and hence a larger percentage of unique words per chapter.

This means that Thoma considered the age of the narrator in each chapter and attempted to tell the story with age-appropriate language. And because stylistic "errors" are thus likely intended by the author, I decided to stay structurally as close to the source language as possible. While I do not discount the possibility of introducing my own errors, many sentences will read "off" because they are supposed to.

Apart from the stylistic separation of juvenile vs. mature diction, Thoma also uses some crude dialect markers to broadly paint his characters. The irate farmer in chapter 1 speaks Bavarian, i.e. a regional dialect, which indicates a lack of education. I tried to approximate this using some features from Wisconsin speech (e.g. "dey" for "they"). The Councilor in chapter 2, on the other hand uses a heavily "umlauted" speech ("Vüloicht, ich woiß es nücht" as opposed to the normally spelled "Vielleicht, ich weiß es nicht") due to permanently pursed lips. This affectation is difficult to mimic in English, so I opted for exaggeratedly pretentious vocabulary instead.

Hopefully, this translation will introduce this book to a wider audience. The reader might get a glimpse of what life was like in rural Germany

towards the end of the nineteenth century. Surely, the passive-aggressive character of the narrator forebodes the real grumbling adult Thoma, but let's not punish the early author for the sins of the elder. The pranks do have a timeless quality and have understandably entertained generations of children.

The text is illustrated with relevant photographs where suitable ones were available. The drawings come from *Simplicissimus*, the weekly satire magazine which Thoma led during the time he wrote his *Rascal Stories*. Their disrespectful drawing style matches that of Thoma's writing.

Ludwig Thoma's Rascal Stories

CHAPTER 1: THE ELEGANT BOY

Der vornehme Knabe

The elegant boy

Zum Scheckbauern ist im Sommer eine Familie gekommen. Die war sehr vornehm, und sie ist aus Preußen gewesen.

This summer, a family came to stay with farmer Scheck. They were very elegant and came from Prussia.

Wie ihr Gepäck gekommen ist, war ich auf der Bahn, und der Stationsdiener hat gesagt, es ist lauter Juchtenleder, die müssen viel Gerstl haben.

When their luggage arrived, I happened to be at the train station, and the station attendant said that it was all Russian leather: they must have lots of dough.

Und meine Mutter hat gesagt, es sind feine Leute, du mußt sie immer grüßen, Ludwig.

And my mother said these are fine people, you always have to greet them, Ludwig.

Er hat einen weißen Bart gehabt, und seine Stiefel haben laut geknarrzt. Sie hat immer Handschuhe angehabt, und wenn es wo naß war auf dem Boden, hat

He had a white beard and his boots were creaking all the time. She always wore gloves, and when the ground was wet, she screamed gosh! and pulled up her dress.

16

sie huh! geschrien und hat ihr Kleid aufgehoben.

Wie sie den ersten Tag da waren, sind sie im Dorf herumgegangen. Er hat die Häuser angeschaut und ist stehengeblieben. Da habe ich gehört, wie er gesagt hat: »Ich möchte nur wissen, von was diese Leute leben.«

Bei uns sind sie am Abend vorbei, wie wir gerade gegessen haben. Meine Mutter hat gegrüßt, und Ännchen auch. Da ist er her gekommen mit seiner Frau und hat gefragt: »Was essen Sie da?«

Wir haben Lunge mit Knödel gegessen, und meine Mutter hat es ihm gesagt.

Da hat er gefragt, ob wir immer Knödel essen, und seine Frau hat uns durch einen Zwicker angeschaut. Es war aber kein rechter Zwicker, sondern er war an einer kleinen Stange, und sie hat ihn auf- und zugemacht.

On their first day here, they took a walk around the village. He looked at the houses and stopped. Then I heard him say: "I just cannot fathom how these people support themselves."

They came by our place in the evening while we were eating. My mother greeted them and so did Annie. He approached us with his wife and asked: "What are you eating there?"

We were having lungs with dumplings, and my mother told him so.

Then he asked if we always ate dumplings, and his wife was looking at us through spectacles. Not the normal kind of spectacles – these were attached to a little stick, and she kept closing and opening them.

1 woman with lorgnette

Meine Mutter sagte zu mir: »Steh auf, Ludwig, und mache den Herrschaften dein Kompliment«, und ich habe es gemacht.

Da hat er zu mir gesagt, was ich bin, und ich habe gesagt, ich bin ein Lateinschüler. Und meine Mutter sagte: »Er war in der ersten Klasse und darf aufsteigen. Im Lateinischen hat er die Note zwei gekriegt.«

Er hat mich auf den Kopf getätschelt und hat gesagt: »Ein gescheiter Junge; du kannst einmal zu uns kommen und mit meinem Arthur spielen. Er ist so alt wie du.«

My mother said to me: "Stand up, Ludwig, take a bow before the gentlemen," and so I did.

Then he asked me what I was, and I told him I was a Latin student. And my mother said: "He was in first grade and is allowed to advance. In Latin, he received a B."

He patted me on the head and said: "A smart boy; you can come to visit us and play with our Arthur. He is your age."

Dann hat er meine Mutter gefragt, wieviel sie Geld kriegt im Monat, und sie ist ganz rot geworden und hat gesagt, daß sie hundert zehn Mark kriegt.

Er hat zu seiner Frau hinübergeschaut und hat gesagt: »Emilie, noch nicht vierzig Taler.«

Und sie hat wieder ihren Zwicker vor die Augen gehalten.

Dann sind sie gegangen, und er hat gesagt, daß man es noch gehört hat: »Ich möchte bloß wissen, von was diese Leute leben.«

Am andern Tag habe ich den Arthur gesehen. Er war aber nicht so groß wie ich und hat lange Haare gehabt bis auf die Schultern und ganz dünne Füße. Das habe ich gesehen, weil er eine Pumphose anhatte. Es war noch ein Mann dabei mit einer Brille auf der Nase. Das war sein Instruktor. Sie sind beim Rafenauer gestanden, wo die Leute Heu gerecht haben.

Der Arthur hat hingedeutet und hat gefragt: »Was tun die da machen?«

Und der Instruktor hat gesagt: »Sie fassen das Heu auf. Wenn es genügend gedörrt ist, werden die Tiere damit gefüttert.«

Then he asked my mother how much money she received per month, and she turned all red and said that she received one hundred ten marks.

He glanced over to his wife and said: "Emilie, not even forty thalers."

And she held her spectacles in front of her eyes again.

Then they left and he said that it was still audible: "I just cannot fathom how these people support themselves."

The next day I saw Arthur. He was not as tall as me, had long hair all the way down to his shoulders and very thin feet. I could see that because he was wearing knickerbockers. There was also a man with glasses on his nose. That was his instructor. They were standing by Rafenauer's, where people were raking hay.

Arthur pointed at them and asked: "What are they doing there?"

And the instructor said: "They are collecting hay. After it has dried enough, they feed it to the animals."

Der Scheck Lorenz war bei mir, und wir haben uns versteckt, weil wir so gelacht haben.

Beim Essen hat meine Mutter gesagt: »Der Herr ist wieder da-gewesen und hat gesagt, du sollst nachmittag seinen Sohn besu-chen.«

Ich sagte, daß ich lieber mit dem Lenz zum Fischen gehe, aber Anna hat mich gleich angefah-ren, daß ich nur mit Bauernlüm-meln herum laufen will, und meine Mutter sagte: »Es ist gut für dich, wenn du mit feinen Leuten zusammen bist. Du kannst Manieren lernen.«

Da hab ich müssen, aber es hat mich nicht gefreut. Ich habe die Hände gewaschen und den schö-nen Rock angezogen, und dann bin ich hin gegangen. Sie waren gerade beim Kaffee, wie ich ge-kommen bin. Der Herr war da und die Frau und ein Mädchen; das war so alt wie unsere Anna, aber schöner angezogen und viel dicker. Der Instruktor war auch da mit dem Arthur.

»Das ist unser junger Freund«, sagte der Herr. »Arthur, gib ihm die Hand!« Und dann fragte er mich: »Nun, habt ihr heute wie-der Knödel gegessen?«

Lorenz Scheck was with me and we went hiding, because we had to laugh so hard.

At lunch, my mother said: "The Gentleman was here again and said you should visit his son this afternoon."

I said that would rather go fish-ing with Lenz, but Anna imme-diately berated me that I just wanted to hang around with country bumpkins, and my mother said: "It is good for you to associate with elegant people. You can learn some manners."

So I had to, but I was not happy about it. I washed my hands and put on the good suit, and then I went. They were just having their coffee when I showed up. The Gentleman was there and the Lady and a girl as old as our Anna, but better dressed and much fatter. The instructor was there as well, together with Ar-thur.

"There is our young friend," said the Gentleman. "Arthur, shake his hand!" And then he asked me: "Now, have you eaten dumplings again today?"

Ich sagte, daß wir keine gegessen haben, und ich habe mich hingesetzt und einen Kaffee gekriegt. Es ist furchtbar fad gewesen. Der Arthur hat nichts geredet und hat mich immer angeschaut, und der Instruktor ist auch ganz still da gesessen.

I said that we had not eaten any, and then I sat down and got a coffee. It was terribly bland. Arthur did not talk and kept looking at me, and the instructor was also sitting there in silence.

Da hat ihn der Herr gefragt, ob Arthur sein Pensum schon fertig hat, und er sagte, ja, es ist fertig; es sind noch einige Fehler darin, aber man merkt schon den Fortschritt.

Then the Gentleman asked him whether Arthur had already completed his workload, and he said yes, it was done; it still contained some mistakes but it already showed noticeable progress.

Da sagte der Herr: »Das ist schön, und Sie können heute nachmittag allein spazierengehen, weil der junge Lateinschüler mit Arthur spielt.«

So the Gentleman said: "That is nice, and you may take a walk by yourself this afternoon, because the young Latin student is going to play with Arthur."

Der Instruktor ist aufgestanden, und der Herr hat ihm eine Zigarre gegeben und gesagt, er soll Obacht geben, weil sie so gut ist.

The instructor got up and the Gentleman gave him a cigar telling him to savor it, because it was so good.

Wie er fort war, hat der Herr gesagt: »Es ist doch ein Glück für diesen jungen Menschen, daß wir ihn mitgenommen haben. Er sieht auf diese Weise sehr viel Schönes.«

After he had left, the Gentleman said: "It is so fortunate for this young person that we took him along. This way he will see many beautiful things."

Aber das dicke Mädchen sagte: »Ich finde ihn gräßlich; er macht Augen auf mich. Ich fürchte, daß er bald dichtet wie der letzte.«

But the fat girl said: "I think he's awful; he keeps eying me up. I'm afraid he's going to start rhyming soon like the last one."

Der Arthur und ich sind bald aufgestanden, und er hat gesagt,

Arthur and I got up, and he said he wanted to show me his toys.

er will mir seine Spielsachen zeigen.

Er hat ein Dampfschiff gehabt. Das wenn man aufgezogen hat, sind die Räder herumgelaufen, und es ist schön geschwommen. Es waren auch viele Bleisoldaten und Matrosen darauf, und Arthur hat gesagt, es ist ein Kriegsschiff und heißt »Preußen«. Aber beim Scheck war kein großes Wasser, daß man sehen kann, wie weit es schwimmt, und ich habe gesagt, wir müssen zum Rafenauer hingehen, da ist ein Weiher, und wir haben viel Spaß dabei.

He had a steam ship. When it was wound up, the wheel turned and it swam nicely. There were also lots of tin soldiers and sailors on it, and Arthur said it was a war ship named "Prussia". But by Scheck's there was no large body of water, so it was impossible to see how far it could swim, and I said that we had to go to Rafenauer's, there was a pond, and we would have lots of fun.

Es hat ihn gleich gefreut, und ich habe das Dampfschiff getragen.

That got him real excited, and I carried the steam ship.

2 steam ship

Sein Papa hat gerufen: »Wo geht ihr denn hin, ihr Jungens ?« Da habe ich ihm gesagt, daß wir das Schiff im Rafenauer seinem Weiher schwimmen lassen.

His Papa called: "Where are you going, you boys?" So I told him we were going to let the ship swim in Rafenauer's pond.

Die Frau sagte: »Du darfst es aber nicht tragen, Arthur. Es ist zu schwer für dich.« Ich sagte,

The Lady said: "But you must not carry it, Arthur. It is too heavy for you." I said that I

daß ich es trage, und sein Papa hat gelacht und hat gesagt: »Das ist ein starker Bayer; er ißt alle Tage Lunge und Knödel. Hahaha!«

would carry it, and his Papa laughed and said: "That is a strong Bavarian; he eats lungs and dumplings all day. Hahaha!"

Wir sind weitergegangen hinter dem Scheck, über die große Wiese.

We walked across the large meadow behind Scheck's.

Der Arthur fragte mich: »Gelt, du bist stark?«

Arthur asked me: "Is it true, are you strong?"

Ich sagte, daß ich ihn leicht hinschmeißen kann, wenn er es probieren will.

I said that I could easily throw him down if he wanted to try.

Aber er traute sich nicht und sagte, er wäre auch gerne so stark, daß er sich von seiner Schwester nichts mehr gefallen lassen muß.

But he did not dare and said he would like to be strong enough not to have to take the abuse from his sister any more.

Ich fragte, ob sie ihn haut.

I asked whether she hit him.

Er sagte nein, aber sie macht sich so gescheit, und wenn er eine schlechte Note kriegt, redet sie darein, als ob es sie was angeht.

He said no, but she always made herself so smart, and when he gets a bad grade, she always meddles as if it were any of her concern.

Ich sagte, das weiß ich schon; das tun alle Mädchen, aber man darf sich nichts gefallen lassen. Es ist ganz leicht, daß man es ihnen vertreibt, wenn man ihnen rechte Angst macht.

I said I already knew about that; all girls did that but you cannot allow it. It is very easy to make them stop if you scare them enough.

Er fragte, was man da tut, und ich sagte, man muß ihnen eine Blindschleiche in das Bett legen. Wenn sie darauffliegen, ist es kalt,

He asked how to do that and I said that you had to put a slow worm into their bed. When they lay down on it, it feels cold, and

und sie schreien furchtbar. Dann versprechen sie einem, daß sie nicht mehr so gescheit sein wollen.

they start screaming terribly. Then they promise to never play smart again.

3 *Blindschleiche- slow worm*

A European lizard without legs. Completely harmless.
pl.wikipedia.org/wiki/user:Marek_bydg

Arthur sagte, er traut sich nicht, weil er vielleicht Schläge kriegt. Ich sagte aber, wenn man sich vor den Schlägen fürchten möchte, darf man nie keinen Spaß haben, und da hat er mir versprochen, daß er es tun will.

Arthur said he did not dare because he might get spanked. But I said if you are afraid of getting slapped you could never have any fun, and he promised me to do it.

Ich habe mich furchtbar gefreut, weil mir das dicke Mädchen gar nicht gefallen hat, und ich dachte, sie wird ihre Augen noch viel stärker aufreißen, wenn sie eine Blindschleiche spürt. Er meinte, ob ich auch gewiß eine finde. Ich sagte, daß ich viele

I was terribly excited, because I did not like the fat girl at all, and I thought she would open her eyes even wider when she feels a slow worm. He asked if I was sure to find one. I said that I could get many, because I knew of a nest in the saw mill.

24

kriegen kann, weil ich in der Sä-gemühle ein Nest weiß.

Und es ist mir eingefallen, ob es nicht vielleicht gut ist, wenn er dem Instruktor auch eine hinein-legt.

And it occurred to me that it would nice to put one into the instructor's bed as well.

Das hat ihm gefallen, und er sagte, er will es gewiß tun, weil sich der Instruktor so fürchtet, daß er vielleicht weggeht.

He liked that and said he would for sure do it, because the in-structor would perhaps be scared enough to leave.

Er fragte, ob ich keinen Instruk-tor habe, und ich sagte, daß meine Mutter nicht so viel Geld hat, daß sie einen zahlen kann.

He asked whether I did not have an instructor, and I said that my mother did not have enough money to pay for one.

Da hat er gesagt: »Das ist wahr. Sie kosten sehr viel, und man hat bloß Verdruß davon. Der letzte, den wir gehabt haben, hat immer Gedichte auf meine Schwester gemacht, und er hat sie unter ihre Kaffeetasse gelegt; da haben wir ihn fortgejagt.«

He said: "That's true. They cost a lot, and you only have trouble with them. Our last one always made poems about my sister, and he put them under her cof-fee cup, so we chased him off."

Ich fragte, warum er Gedichte gemacht hat und warum er keine hat machen dürfen.

I asked why he had made poems and why he had not been al-lowed to do so.

Da sagte er: »Du bist aber dumm. Er war doch verliebt in meine Schwester, und sie hat es gleich gemerkt, weil er sie immer so angeschaut hat. Deswegen ha-ben wir ihn fortjagen müssen.«

So he said: "You are so dumb. He was in love with my sister, and she realized right away, be-cause he kept looking at her like that. That's why we had to chase him off."

Ich dachte, wie dumm es ist, daß sich einer so plagen mag wegen dem dicken Mädchen, und ich

I thought how dumb it was that someone would take so much trouble because of the fat girl, and that I sure did not want to

möchte sie gewiß nicht anschauen und froh sein, wenn sie nicht dabei ist.

Dann sind wir an den Weiher beim Rafenauer gekommen, und wir haben das Dampfschiff hineingetan. Die Räder sind gut gegangen, und es ist ein Stück weit geschwommen.

Wir sind auch hineingewatet, und der Arthur hat immer geschrien: »Hurra! Gebt's ihnen, Jungens! Klar zum Gefecht! Drauf und dran, Jungens, gebt ihnen noch eine Breitseite! Brav, Kinder!« Er hat furchtbar geschrien, daß er ganz rot geworden ist, und ich habe ihn gefragt, was das ist.

Er sagte, es ist eine Seeschlacht, und er ist ein preußischer Admiral. Sie spielen es immer in Köln; zuerst ist er bloß Kapitän gewesen, aber jetzt ist er Admiral, weil er viele Schlachten gewonnen hat.

Dann hat er wieder geschrien: »Beidrehen! Beidrehen! Hart an Backbord halten! Feuer! Sieg! Sieg!«

Ich sagte: »Das gefällt mir gar nicht; es ist eine Dummheit, weil sich nichts rührt. Wenn es eine Schlacht ist, muß es krachen. Wir sollen Pulver hineintun, dann ist es lustig.« Er sagte, daß er nicht

look at her and that I was glad she was not along.

Then we arrived at the pond by Rafenauer's, and we put the ship to water. The wheels turned well, and it swam for a bit.

We also waded in, and Arthur kept yelling: "Hurray! Give it to them, boys! Ready for battle! On, boys, give them another broadside! Well done, kids!" He was yelling around like crazy, turning all red, and I asked him what that was about.

He said it was a sea battle, and he was a Prussian admiral. They always played this in Cologne; at first, he had only been a captain, but now he was an admiral, because he had won so many battles.

Then he started yelling again: "Heave to! Heave to! Keep hard to port! Fire! Victory! Victory!"

I said: "I don't like this at all; it's dumb, because nothing is happening. If it is a battle, it needs to crash. We have to put powder in, then it'll be fun." He said he was not allowed to play with powder,

mit Pulver spielen darf, weil es gefährlich ist. Alle Jungen in Köln machen es ohne Pulver.

because it was so danger… boys in Cologne do it w… powder.

Ich habe ihn aber ausgelacht, weil er doch kein Admiral ist, wenn er nicht schießt.

But I laughed at him, because he was no admiral if he did not shoot.

Und ich habe gesagt, ich tue es, wenn er sich nicht traut; ich mache den Kapitän, und er muß bloß kommandieren.

And I said I would do it if he did not dare; I would make the captain, and he just needed to give commands.

Da ist er ganz lustig gewesen und hat gesagt, das möchte er. Ich muß aber streng folgen, weil er mein Vorgesetzter ist, und Feuer geben, wenn er schreit.

Then he was all excited and said he wanted to do that. But I had to strictly follow orders, because he was my superior, and I would have to fire when he yells.

Ich habe ein Paket Pulver bei mir gehabt. Das habe ich immer, weil ich so oft Speiteufel mache. Und ein Stück Zündschnur habe ich auch dabei gehabt.

I had a bag of powder on me. I always had one, because I often made fountain fireworks. And I also had a piece of fuse.

Wir haben das Dampfschiff hergezogen. Es waren Kanonen darauf, aber sie haben kein Loch gehabt. Da habe ich probiert, ob man vielleicht anders schießen kann. Ich meinte, man soll das Verdeck aufheben und drunter das Pulver tun. Dann geht der Rauch bei den Luken heraus, und man glaubt auch, es sind Kanonen darin.

We pulled the steam ship close. There were cannons on top, but they did not have any holes. So I looked for a different way to shoot. I thought we should lift the deck and put the powder underneath. Then the smoke would come out the hatches and you would think there were cannons inside.

Das habe ich getan. Ich habe aber das ganze Paket Pulver hineingeschüttet, damit es stärker raucht. Dann habe ich das Verdeck wieder darauf getan und die

That is what I did. I poured the whole bag of powder in to make it smoke more. Then I put the deck back on and stuck the fuse through a hole.

Zündschnur durch ein Loch gesteckt.

Arthur fragte, ob es recht knallen wird, und ich sagte, ich glaube schon, daß es einen guten Schuß tut. Da ist er geschwind hinter einen Baum und hat gesagt, jetzt geht die Schlacht an.

Arthur asked whether it would make a nice bang and I said that I thought it would give a nice shot. So he quickly went behind a tree and said the battle was on.

Und er hat wieder geschrien: »Hurra! Gebt's ihnen, tapferer Kapitän!«

And again he yelled: "Hurray! Give it to them, brave captain!"

Ich habe das Dampfschiff aufge-dreht und gehalten, bis die Zündschnur gebrannt hat.

I wound up the steam ship and held it until the fuse was lit.

Dann habe ich ihm einen Stoß gegeben, und die Räder sind ge-gangen, und die Zündschnur hat geraucht.

Then I gave it a good push, and the wheels were turning, and the fuse was smoking.

Es war lustig, und der Arthur hat sich auch furchtbar gefreut und hinter dem Baum immer kom-mandiert.

It was fun, and Arthur was also terribly excited, and he kept shouting commands behind the tree.

Er fragte, warum es nicht knallt. Ich sagte, es knallt schon, wenn die Zündschnur einmal bis zum Pulver hinbrennt.

He asked why there was no boom. I said it would bang as soon as the fuse had burnt all the way to the powder.

Da hat er seinen Kopf vorge-streckt und hat geschrien: »Gebt Feuer auf dem Achterdeck!«

So he put his head out and screamed: "Give fire on the quarterdeck!"

Auf einmal hat es einen furcht-baren Krach getan und hat ge-zischt, und ein dicker Rauch ist auf dem Wasser gewesen. Ich habe gemeint, es ist etwas bei mir vorbei geflogen, aber Arthur hat

Suddenly there was a terrible bang and it hissed, and a huge plume of smoke appeared over the water. I thought something flew by me, but Arthur already started some awful wailing, and

schon gräßlich geheult, und er hat seinen Kopf gehalten. Es war aber nicht arg. Er hat bloß ein bißchen geblutet an der Stirne, weil ihn etwas getroffen hat. Ich glaube, es war ein Bleisoldat.

Ich habe ihn abgewischt, und er hat gefragt, wo sein Dampfschiff ist. Es war aber nichts mehr da; bloß der vordere Teil war noch da und ist auf dem Wasser geschwommen. Das andere ist alles in die Luft geflogen. Er hat geweint, weil er geglaubt hat, daß sein Vater schimpft, wenn kein Schiff nicht mehr da ist. Aber ich habe gesagt, wir sagen, daß die Räder so gelaufen sind, und es ist fortgeschwommen, oder er sagt gar nichts und geht erst heim, wenn es dunkel ist. Dann weiß es niemand, und wenn ihn wer fragt, wo das Schiff ist, sagt er, es ist droben, aber er mag nicht damit spielen. Und wenn eine Woche vorbei ist, sagt er, es ist auf einmal nicht mehr da. Vielleicht ist es gestohlen worden.

Der Arthur sagte, er will es so machen und warten, bis es dunkel wird.

Wie wir das geredet haben, da hat es hinter uns Spektakel gemacht.

Ich habe geschwind umgeschaut, und da habe ich auf einmal gese-

he was holding his head. But it was not bad. He was only bleeding a little bit from his forehead, because something had hit him. I think it was a lead soldier.

I wiped him off and he asked where his steam ship was. It was gone; only the front part was still there, swimming on the water. The rest had been blown to pieces. He was crying because he thought his father would scold him if the ship was gone. But I said we should say that the wheels had been turning so much and that it had swum away, or that he should not say anything and not go home until it was dark. Then nobody knows about it and if someone asks where the ship is, then he says it is upstairs, but he does not want to play with it. And when a week has passed, he says that it has suddenly disappeared. Maybe it got stolen.

Arthur said he wanted to do that and wait until dark.

As we were talking, a commotion started behind us.

I quickly turned around and saw Rafenauer running towards us. He was yelling: "Now I got yous

hen, wie der Rafenauer hergelaufen ist. Er hat geschrien: »Hab ich enk, ihr Saububen, ihr miserabligen!«

dang scoundrels, yous miserables!"

Ich bin gleich davon, bis ich zum Heustadel gekommen bin. Da habe ich mich geschwind versteckt und hingeschaut. Der Arthur ist stehengeblieben, und der Rafenauer hat ihm die Ohrfeigen gegeben. Er ist furchtbar grob.

I took off immediately all the way to the hay barn. There I quickly hid and looked. Arthur was standing there and Rafenauer was slapping him in the face. He was terribly rough.

Und er hat immer geschrien: »De Saububen zünden noch mei Haus o. Und meine Äpfel stehlen s', und meine Zwetschgen stehlen s', und mei Haus sprengen s' in d' Luft!«

And he kept screaming: "Dese dang scoundrels are gonna put fire to mine house. An dey're stealin mine apples, an dey're stealin mine plums, an dey're blowin up mine house!"

Er hat ihm jedesmal eine Watschen gegeben, daß es geknallt hat.

And every time he slapped him that it banged.

Ich habe schon gewußt, daß er einen Zorn auf uns hat, weil ich und der Lenz ihm so oft seine Äpfel stehlen, und er kann uns nicht erwischen.

I already knew that he was angry with us, because I and Lenz often stole his apples and he cannot catch us.

Aber den Arthur hat er jetzt erwischt, und er hat alle Prügel gekriegt.

But now he got Arthur, and he received all the thrashing.

Wie der Rafenauer fertig war, ist er fortgegangen. Aber dann ist er stehengeblieben und hat gesagt: »Du Herrgottsakerament!« und ist wieder umgekehrt und hat ihm nochmal eine hineingehauen.

When Rafenauer was done, he started walking away. But then he stopped and said: "Damn yous!" and he turned around and slapped Arthur again.

Der Arthur hat furchtbar geweint und hat immer geschrien: »Ich sage es meinem Papa!« Es wäre gescheiter gewesen, wenn er fortgelaufen wäre; der Rafenauer kann nicht nachkommen, weil er so schnauft. Man muß immer um die Bäume herumlaufen, dann bleibt er gleich stehen und sagt: »Ich erwisch enk schon noch einmal.«

Ich und der Lenz wissen es; aber der Arthur hat es nicht gewußt.

Er hat mich gedauert, weil er so geweint hat, und wie der Rafenauer fort war, bin ich hingelaufen und habe gesagt, er soll sich nichts daraus machen. Aber er hat nicht aufgehört und hat immer geschrien: »Du bist schuld; ich sage es meinem Papa.«

Da habe ich mich aber geärgert und ich habe gesagt, daß ich nichts dafür kann, wenn er so dumm ist.

Da hat er gesagt, ich habe das Schiff kaputtgemacht, und ich habe so geknallt, daß der Bauer gekommen ist und er Schläge gekriegt hat.

Und er ist schnell fortgelaufen und hat geweint, daß man es weit gehört hat. Ich möchte mich schämen, wenn ich so heulen könnte wie ein Mädchen. Und er hat gesagt, er ist ein Admiral.

Arthur was crying terribly and was yelling: "I will tell my Papa!" It would have been smarter for him to run away; Rafenauer cannot go after him, because he wheezes so much. You just have to run around the trees and then he stops and says: "I'm going to get you someday!"

I and Lenz know this, but Arthur had no idea.

I felt bad because he was crying to much, and when Rafenauer was gone, I ran to him and said he should not worry about it. But he did not stop and kept yelling: "It is your fault; I will tell my Papa."

That made me angry and I said that it was not my fault that he was so dumb.

So he said that I had broken his ship and I had banged to much that the farmer had come and he had been beaten.

And he quickly ran off and was crying that you could hear it from far away. I would have been ashamed to wail like this like a girl. And he said he was an admiral.

Ich dachte, es ist gut, wenn ich nicht gleich heimgehe, sondern ein bißchen warte.

I thought it would be good not to go home right away, but to wait a bit.

Wie es dunkel war, bin ich heim gegangen, und ich bin beim Scheck ganz still vorbei, daß mich niemand gemerkt hat.

When it was dark, I went home, and I snuck by Scheck's, so that nobody would notice me.

Der Herr war im Gartenhaus und die Frau und das dicke Mädchen. Der Scheck war auch dabei. Ich habe hineingeschaut, weil ein Licht gebrannt hat. Ich glaube, sie haben von mir geredet. Der Herr hat immer den Kopf geschüttelt und hat gesagt: »Wer hätte es gedacht! Ein solcher Lausejunge!« Und das dicke Mädchen hat gesagt: »Er will, daß mir Arthur Schlangen ins Bett legt. Hat man so was gehört?«

The Gentleman was in the garden house, and the Lady and the fat girl. Scheck were there as well. I looked inside, because a light was on. I think they were talking about me. The Gentleman kept shaking his head and said: "Who would have thought! Such a rascal!" And the fat girl said: "He wants Arthur to put snakes into my bed. Have you ever heard such a thing?"

Ich bin nicht mehr eingeladen worden, aber wenn mich der Herr sieht, hebt er immer seinen Stock auf und ruft: »Wenn ich dich mal erwische!« Ich bin aber nicht so dumm wie sein Arthur, daß ich stehenbleibe.

So I never got invited again, but when the Gentleman sees me, he always lifts his cane and calls: "When I get you!" But I am not as dumb as Arthur and would not stick around.

CHAPTER 2: SUMMER VACATIONS

In den Ferien

Summer vacations

Es ist die große Vakanz gewesen, und sie hat schon vier Wochen gedauert. Meine Mutter hat oft geseufzt, daß wir so lange frei haben, weil alle Tage etwas passiert, und meine Schwester hat gesagt, daß ich die Familie in einen schlechten Ruf bringe.

We had the long vacation and were already four weeks into it. My mother kept sighing that we were off for too long, because every day something was happening, and my sister said that I would give the family a bad reputation.

Da ist einmal der Lehrer Wagner zu uns auf Besuch gekommen. Er kommt öfter, weil meine Mutter soviel vom Obst versteht, und er kann sich mit ihr unterhalten.

Once, teacher Wagner came to visit us. He comes over frequently, because my mother knows a lot about fruit, and he can have a conversation with her.

Er hat erzählt, daß seine Pfirsiche schön werden und daß es ihm Freude macht.

He told us that his peaches will be beautiful and that he enjoys it.

Und dann hat er auch gesagt, daß die Volksschule in zwei Tagen schon wieder angeht und seine Vakanz vorbei ist.

And then he also said that the common school was starting again in two days and his vacations would be over.

Meine Mutter hat gesagt, sie möchte froh sein, wenn das Gymnasium auch schon angeht, aber sie muß es noch drei Wochen aushalten.

Der Lehrer sagte: »Ja, ja, es ist nicht gut, wenn die Burschen so lange frei haben. Sie kommen auf alles mögliche.«

Und dann ist er gegangen. Zufällig habe ich an diesem Tage eine Forelle gestohlen gehabt, und der Fischer ist zornig zu uns gelaufen und hat geschrien, er zeigt es an, wenn er nicht drei Mark dafür kriegt.

Da bin ich furchtbar geschimpft worden, aber meine Schwester hat gesagt: »Was hilft es? Morgen fängt er etwas anderes an, und kein Mensch mag mehr mit uns verkehren. Gestern hat mich der Amtsrichter so kalt gegrüßt, wie er vorbeigegangen ist. Sonst bleibt er immer stehen und fragt, wie es uns geht.«

Meine Mutter hat gesagt, daß etwas geschehen muß, sie weiß noch nicht, was.

Auf einmal ist ihnen eingefallen, ob ich vielleicht in der Vakanz in die Volksschule gehen kann, der Herr Lehrer tut ihnen gewiß den Gefallen.

Ich habe gesagt, das geht nicht, weil ich schon in die zweite

My mother said she would be glad if Latin school would also start, but she still had to endure three more weeks.

The teacher said: "Yes, it is not good that the guys have off for such a long time. They cook up all kinds of things."

And then he left. These days, I happened to have stolen a trout and the angry fisherman came running to us and screamed that he would call the police if he did not get his three marks for it.

I got a terrible scolding, but my sister said: "What good is it? Tomorrow, he'll start something else and nobody will want to have anything to do with us anymore. Yesterday, the judge gave me such a cold greeting when he went by. Usually, he stops and asks how we are doing."

My mother said that something needed to happen but she did not know what yet.

Suddenly it occurred to them that I could possibly visit the common school during my vacations, the teacher would surely do them this favor.

I told them that was impossible, because I already went into the

Klasse von der Lateinschule komme, und wenn es die anderen erfahren, ist es eine furchtbare Schande vor meinen Kommilitonen. Lieber will ich nichts mehr anfangen und sehr fleißig sein.

Meine liebe Mutter sagte zu meiner Schwester: »Du hörst es, daß er jetzt anders werden will, und wenn es für ihn doch so peinlich ist wegen der Kolimitonen, wollen wir noch einmal warten.«

Sie kann sich keine lateinischen Worte merken.

Ich war froh, daß es so vorbeigegangen ist, und ich habe mich recht zusammengenommen.

Einen Tag ist es gut gegangen, aber am Mittwoch habe ich es nicht mehr ausgehalten.

Neben uns wohnt der Geheimrat Bischof in der Sommerfrische. Seine Frau kann mich nicht leiden, und wenn ich bloß an den Zaun hinkomme, schreit sie zu ihrer Magd: »Elis, geben Sie acht, der Lausbube ist da.«

Sie haben eine Angorakatze; die darf immer dabeisitzen, wenn sie Kaffee trinken im Freien, und die Frau Geheimrat fragt: »Mag Miezchen ein bißchen Milch? Mag Miezchen vielleicht auch ein bißchen Honig?«

second year at Latin school, and if the others got wind of this, it would be a huge embarrassment in front of my school associates. I would much prefer to not start any trouble anymore and be very diligent.

My dear mother said to my sister: "There you hear it that he wants to change now, and since it would be so embarrassing for him because of the other assoosiates, then we want to wait one more time."

She cannot remember Latin words.

I was glad that this had passed me by, and I really pulled myself together.

This went well for one day, but on Wednesday, I could not take it anymore.

Next door, Councilor Bischof stayed for his summer retreat. His wife cannot stand me and when I just come near their fence, she yells to her maid: "Elis, watch out, the rascal is here."

The have an Angora cat that is always allowed to sit with them when they drink their coffee outside, and then Mrs Councilor asks: "Would Kitty like a little milk? Would Kitty like a bit of honey, too?"

Als wenn sie ja sagen könnte oder ein kleines Kind wäre.

Am Mittwoch ist die Katze bei uns herüben gewesen, und unsere Magd hat sie gefüttert. Da habe ich sie genommen, wie es niemand gesehen hat, und habe sie eingesperrt im Stall, wo ich früher zwei Königshasen hatte.

Dann habe ich aufgepaßt, wie sie Kaffee getrunken haben. Die Frau Geheimrat war schon da und hat gerufen: »Miezi! Miezi! Elis, haben Sie Miezchen nicht gesehen?«

Aber die Magd hat es nicht gewußt, und sie haben sich hingesetzt, und ich habe hinter dem Vorhang hinübergeschaut.

Dann hat die Frau Geheimrat zu ihrem Mann gesagt: »Eugen, hast du Miezchen nicht gesehen?«

Und er hat gesagt: »Vüloicht, ich woiß es nücht.« Und dann hat er wieder in der Zeitung gelesen.

Aber die Frau Geheimrat war ganz nachdenklich, und wie sie ein Butterbrot geschmiert hat, hat sie gesagt: »Ich kann mir nicht denken, wo Miezchen bleibt. Sie fängt doch keine Mäuse nicht?«

Indes bin ich geschwind in den Stall und habe die Katze genommen. Ich habe ihr an den

As if it could say yes or were a little child.

On Wednesday, the cat came over to us and our maid gave her something to eat. Then I took her when nobody was looking and I locked her into the cage in which I used to keep two large rabbits.

Then I observed them take their coffee. Mr Councilor was already there and was calling: "Kitty! Kitty! Elis, have you not seen Kitty?"

But the maid did not know anything and sat down, and I was watching from behind the curtain.

Then, Mrs Councilor said to her husband: "Eugen, have you not seen Kitty?"

And he said: "Perchance, I am incognizant." And then he went back to reading his newspaper.

But Mrs Councilor was deep in thought, and as she was buttering a slice of bread, she said: "I cannot imagine where Kitty might be. She does not catch any mice, does she?"

Meanwhile, I quickly went into the barn and got the cat. I tied a jumping cracker to her tail and

Schweif einen Pulverfrosch gebunden und bin hinten an das Haus vom Geheimrat am Zaun und habe den Frosch angezündet. Dann habe ich die Katze freigelassen. Sie ist gleich durch den Zaun geschloffen und furchtbar gelaufen.

took her to the fence behind the Councilor's house. There I lit the fuse and let the cat go. She immediately slipped through the fence and ran like crazy.

4 Pulverfrosch – jumping cracker

Die Magd hat geschrien: »Frau Geheimrat, Mieze kommt schon.« Und dann habe ich die Stimme von ihr gehört, wie sie gesagt hat: »Wo ist nur mein Kätzchen? Da bist du ja! Aber was hat das Tierchen am Schweif?« Dann hat es furchtbar gekracht und gezischt, und sie haben geschrien und die Tassen am Boden hingeschmissen, und wie es still war, hat der Geheimrat gesagt: »Das üst wüder düser ruchlose Lauspube gewösen.«

The maid yelled: "Mrs Councilor, Kitty is coming." And then I heard her voice, as she was saying: "Where is my Kitty? There you are! But what has the little animal on her tail?" Then there was a terrible banging and hissing and they were screaming and tossed their cups to the ground, and when it was quiet again, the Councilor said: "Certainly, that most wicked rascal precipitated this again!"

Ich habe mich im Zimmer von meiner Schwester versteckt; da kann man in unseren Garten hinunterschauen. Meine Mutter und Anna haben auch Kaffee getrunken, und meine liebe Mutter sagte gerade: »Siehst du, Ännchen, Ludwig ist nicht so schlimm; man muß ihn nur zu

I went hiding in my sister's room; there you can look down into our yard. My mother and Anna were also drinking coffee and my dear mother was just saying: "See, Annie, Ludwig is not so bad; you just need to know how to handle him. Yesterday, he studied all day, and it is good

behandeln verstehen. Gestern hat er den ganzen Tag gelernt, und es ist gut, daß wir ihn nicht vor seinen Kolimitonen blamiert haben.«

Und Anna sagte: »Ich möchte bloß wissen, warum der Herr Amtsrichter nicht stehengeblieben ist.«

Jetzt ist auf einmal am Eingang von unserem Garten der Geheimrat und die Frau Geheimrat gewesen, und meine Mutter sagte: »Ännchen, sitzt meine Haube nicht schief? Ich glaube gar, Geheimrats machen uns Besuch.«

Und sie ist aufgestanden und ihnen entgegengegangen, und ich hörte, daß sie gesagt hat: »Nein, das ist lieb von Ihnen, daß Sie kommen.« Aber der Geheimrat hat ein Gesicht gemacht, als wenn er mit einer Leiche geht, und sie ist ganz rot gewesen und hat den abgebrannten Frosch in der Hand gehabt und hat erzählt, daß die Katze jetzt wahnsinnig ist und drei Tassen kaputt sind. Und daß es niemand anderer getan hat wie ich. Da sind meiner Mutter die Tränen heruntergelaufen, und der Geheimrat hat gesagt: »Woinen Sü nur, gute Frau! Woinen Sü über Ühren mißratenen Sohn!« Und dann haben sie verlangt, daß meine

that we did not embarrass him in front of his assoosiates."

And Anna said: "I'm still wondering why Mr Judge did not stay to chat."

Suddenly, the Councilor and Mrs Councilor appeared at the gate of our yard, and my mother said: "Annie, does my bonnet sit right? I believe the Councilors are coming to visit."

And she got up and went to meet them, and I heard her saying: "Now, how nice of you to stop by." But the councilor made a face as if he were walking with a corpse, and she was all red and held the burnt-up fire cracker in her hand and told that the cat was out of her mind now and three cups were broken. And that none other than me had done this. There, tears started running down my mother's face and the Councilor said: "Go ahead and lament, good woman! Shed Your tears over Your wayward offspring!" And then they demanded that my mother pay the cups, and each cost two

Mutter die Tassen bezahlt, und eine kostet zwei Mark, weil es so gutes Porzellan war.

Ich bin furchtbar zornig geworden, wie ich gesehen habe, daß meine alte Mutter den kleinen, alten Geldbeutel herausgetan hat, und ihre Hände waren ganz zittrig, wie sie das Geld aufgezählt hat.

Die Frau Geheimrat hat es geschwind eingesteckt und hat gesagt, das Schrecklichste ist, daß die arme Katze wahnsinnig geworden ist, aber sie wollen es nicht anzeigen aus Rücksicht auf meine Mutter. Dann sind sie gegangen, und er hat noch gesagt: »Der Hümmel prüft Sü hart mit Ührem Künde.«

Ich habe noch länger in den Garten hinuntergeschaut. Da ist meine Mutter am Tisch gesessen und hat sich mit ihrem Sacktuch die Tränen abgewischt, aber es sind immer neue gekommen, und bei Ännchen auch. Das Butterbrot ist auf dem Teller gewesen, und sie haben es nicht mehr essen mögen. Ich bin ganz traurig geworden, und ich bin fort, daß sie mich nicht gesehen haben.

Ich habe gedacht, wie es gemein ist von dem Geheimrat, daß er das Geld genommen hat, und wie ich ihm dafür etwas antun

marks, because it was such good porcelain.

I became terribly furious when I saw my old mother pull out her little old purse and count out the money with shaky hands.

Mrs Councilor quickly pocketed the money and said that the worst was for her cat to have gone mad, but she did not want to report this out of consideration for my mother. Then they left and he said in passing: "The Heavens are assessing Your faith with Your progeny."

I kept looking down into the yard for a while. There, my mother sat at the table and wiped off her tears with her sackcloth, but more kept coming, and same for Annie. Their buttered bread lay on their plates, and they did not feel like eating it any more. I got real sad and left without them seeing me.

I thought how mean the Councilor had been to take the money and that I had to do something to him for that. I would have

muß. Ich möchte die Katze kaputt machen, daß es niemand merkt, und ihr den Schweif abschneiden. Wenn sie dann ruft: »Wo ist denn nur unser Miezchen?«, schmeiße ich den Schweif über den Zaun hinüber. Aber ich muß mich noch besinnen, wie ich es mache, daß es niemand merkt. Da bin ich wieder lustig geworden, weil ich gedacht habe, was sie für ein Gesicht machen wird, wenn sie bloß mehr den Schweif sieht. Dann bin ich heim zum essen gegangen. Anna ist schon an der Tür gestanden und hat gesagt, daß ich allein essen muß in meinem Zimmer und daß ich morgen in die Schule gehen muß. Der Herr Lehrer Wagner hat es angenommen und hat versprochen, daß er mit mir streng ist.

Ich habe schimpfen gewollt, weil es doch eine Schande ist, wenn ein Lateinschüler mit den dummen Schulkindern zusammensitzt, aber ich habe gedacht, daß meine Mutter so geweint hat.

Und da habe ich mir alles gefallen lassen.

Ich bin am andern Tag in die Schule gegangen. Es war bloß ein Zimmer, und da waren alle Klassen darin, und auf der einen Seite waren die Buben und auf der anderen die Mädchen.

liked to destroy the cat without anybody noticing and to cut off her tail. When she then calls "Now, where is our Kitty?", I would throw the tail over the fence. But I had to think hard about how to do this without anybody noticing. This got me into a better mood, because I imagined her face when she sees just the tail. Then I went home to eat. Anna stood by the door and said that I had to eat in my room by myself and that I had to go to school in the morning. Mr Teacher Wagner had agreed and promised to be strict with me.

I wanted to grumble, because it was such an embarrassment for a Latin student to sit with the dumb school kids, but I remembered how my mother had cried.

And so I let it all happen.

The next day, I went to school. It was just one room, and all grades were in there together, and the boys were on one side and the girls on the other.

Wie ich gekommen bin, hat mich der Lehrer in die erste Bank gesetzt. Dann hat er gesagt, daß sich die Kinder Mühe geben sollen, weil heute ein großer Gelehrter unter ihnen sitzt, der Lateinisch kann.

When I arrived, the teacher put me in the front bench. Then he said that all children should try hard, because today there was a great scholar among them who knows Latin.

5 class picture around 1909

Das hat mich verdrossen, weil die Kinder gelacht haben. Aber ich habe es mir nicht merken lassen. Einer hat ein Lesestück vorlesen müssen. Es hat geheißen »Der Abend« und ist so angegangen: »Die Sonne geht zur Ruhe, und am Himmel kommt der Abendstern. Die Vöglein verstummen mit ihrem lieblichen Gesange; nur die Grillen zirpen im Felde. Da geht der fleißige Bauersmann heim. Sein Hund

I bristled when all children were laughing. But I did not show it. One of them had to read a piece aloud. It was called "The Evening" and started out like this: "The sun goes to rest, and the evening star rises to heaven. The little birds stop their lovely song; only the crickets chirp in the field. Then the hardworking farmer goes home. His dog barks happily, and the children jump to greet him." This is how it went

bellt freudig, und die Kinder springen ihm entgegen.« So ist es weitergegangen. Es war furchtbar dumm, und ich habe gedacht, was es für eine Schande ist für einen Lateinschüler, daß er dabeisitzen muß.

Der Lehrer sagte, die Kinder von der siebenten Klasse müssen es nun aus dem Kopfe schreiben, und er ladet den Herrn Lateinschüler auch ein.

Er hat mir eine Tafel und einen Griffel gegeben, und dann sagte er, daß er eine halbe Stunde in die Kirche fort muß, und daß die Furtner Marie die Aufsicht hat. Sie war auch von der siebenten Klasse und die Tochter von einem Bauern, der nicht weit von uns ein Haus hat. Da bin ich noch zorniger geworden, daß ich einem Mädel folgen soll.

on. It was terribly dumb, and I thought it was a shame for a Latin student to sit through this.

The teacher said that the children from seventh grade now had to write from memory, and he also invited Mr Latin student to participate.

He gave me slate and stylus, and then he said that he had to go to church for half an hour and that Furtner's Marie would be in charge. She was also in seventh grade and the daughter of a farmer who had a house near ours. I was even madder now that I had to follow a girl.

6 Tafel und Griffel – slate and stylus

children used these to practice writing, see
https://de.wikipedia.org/wiki/Schreibtafel
https://en.wikipedia.org/wiki/Slate_(writing)

Wie der Lehrer draußen war, habe ich den Leitner, der neben mir gesessen ist, ganz ruhig gefragt, ob er heute nachmittag zum Fischen mitgehen will.

As soon as the teacher was outside, I calmly asked Leitner, who was sitting next to me, whether he wanted to go fishing with me this afternoon.

Da hat die Furtner Marie gerufen: »Ruhig! Wenn du noch einmal schwätzest, wirst du aufgeschrieben.«

Then Marie Furtner yelled: "Quiet! If you talk one more time, I will write you up!"

»Entschuldigen Sie, Fräulein Lehrerin«, habe ich gesagt, »ich will es nicht mehr tun.«

"I apologize, Miss Teacher," I said, "I won't do it again."

43

Dann habe ich einen Schlüssel aus der Tasche gezogen und habe probiert, ob er noch pfeift.

Then I pulled a key out of my pocket and tried whether it could still whistle.

7 hollow key

Da ist die Furtner Marie zur Tafel hinaus und hat hingeschrieben: »Thoma hat gepfiffen.«

So Marie Furtner went up to the chalk board and wrote: "Thoma whistled."

Ich bin aufgestanden und habe gesagt: »Entschuldigen Sie, Fräulein Lehrerin, was muß ich denn machen, daß Sie mich nicht aufschreiben?«

I got up and said: "Excuse me, Miss Teacher, what do I need to do so that you don't write me up?"

Sie sagte, daß ich den Aufsatz »Der Abend« schreiben muß.

She said that I should write down the "Evening" story.

Da habe ich geschwind etwas geschrieben, und dann bin ich wieder aufgestanden und habe gesagt: »Entschuldigen Sie, Fräulein Lehrerin, darf ich es nicht vorlesen, daß Sie mir sagen, ob es recht ist?«

So I quickly wrote something, and then I stood up again and said: "Excuse me, Miss Teacher, could I read it out loud, so you can tell me if it is correct?"

Da ist die dumme Gans stolz gewesen, daß sie einem Lateinschüler etwas sagen muß, und sie hat gesagt:

There the dumb goose got all proud that she had to tell a Latin student something, and she said:

»Ja, du darfst es vorlesen.«

"Yes, you may read it out loud."

Da habe ich recht laut gelesen:

So I read quite loudly:

»Die Sonne geht zur Ruhe. Der Abendstern ist auf dem Himmel.

"The sun settles down. The evening star is up in the sky. All

44

Vor dem Wirtshause ist es still. Auf einmal geht die Tür auf, und der Hausknecht wirft einen Bauersmann hinaus. Er ist betrunken. Es ist der Furtner Marie ihr Vater.«

Da haben alle Kinder gelacht, und die Furtner hat zu heulen angefangen. Sie ist wieder an die Tafel hin und hat geschrieben: »Thoma war ungezogen.« Das hat sie dreimal unterstrichen. Ich bin aus meiner Bank gegangen und habe den Schwamm genommen und habe ihre Schrift ausgewischt.

Und dann habe ich die Furtner Marie bei ihrem Zopf gepackt und habe sie gebeutelt, und zuletzt habe ich ihr eine Ohrfeige hineingehauen, damit sie weiß, daß man einen Lateinschüler nicht aufschreibt.

Jetzt ist der Lehrer gekommen, und er war zornig, wie er alles erfahren hat. Er sagte, daß er nur wegen meiner Mutter mich nicht gleich hinauswirft, aber daß er mich zwei Stunden nach der Schule einsperrt. Das hat er auch getan. Wie die Kinder fort waren, habe ich dableiben müssen, und der Lehrer hat die Tür mit dem Schlüssel zugesperrt. Es war schon elf Uhr, und ich habe furchtbar Hunger gehabt, und ich habe auch gedacht, was es für

is quiet in front of the tavern. Suddenly the door opens and the keeper's hand throws out a farmer. He is drunk. It is the father of Furtner's Marie."

All of the children started laughing, and Furtner began to cry. She went back to the black board and wrote: "Thoma was naughty again." She underlined it three times. So I got up from my bench and took the sponge and erased her writing.

And then I grabbed Furtner's Marie by her braid and shook her about, and finally I slapped her across the face, so she would know not to write up a Latin student.

Now the teacher came and was angry when he learned about everything. He said that my mother was the only reason he did not expel me immediately, but that he would lock me up for two hours after school. That is what he did. After the children left, I had to stay and the teacher locked the door with the key. It was eleven o'clock already, and I was terribly hungry, and I also thought that it was shameful for

eine Schande ist, daß ich in einer Volksschule eingesperrt bin.

Da habe ich geschaut, ob ich nicht durchbrennen kann und vielleicht beim Fenster hinunterspringen. Aber es war im ersten Stock und zu hoch, und es waren Steine unten. Da schaute ich auf der andern Seite, wo der Garten war. Wenn man auf die Erde springt, tut es vielleicht nicht weh. Ich machte das Fenster auf und dachte, ob ich es probiere. Da habe ich auf einmal gesehen, daß an der Mauer die Latten für das Spalierobst sind, und ich habe gedacht, daß sie mich schon tragen.

Ich bin langsam hinausgestiegen und habe die Füße ganz vorsichtig auf die Latten gestellt. Sie haben mich gut getragen, und wie ich gesehen habe, daß es nicht gefährlich ist, da ist mir eingefallen, daß ich die Pfirsiche mitnehmen kann. Ich habe alle Taschen vollgesteckt und den Hut auch.

Dann bin ich erst heim und legte die Pfirsiche in meinen Kasten.

Am Nachmittag ist ein Brief vom Herrn Lehrer gekommen, daß ich die Schule nicht mehr betreten darf.

Da war ich froh.

me to be locked up in a common school.

So I checked whether I would be able to escape, perhaps by jumping out of the window. But it was on the second floor and too high, and there were rocks down below. So I looked out the other side, where the garden was. When you jump onto dirt, it might not hurt that much. I opened the window and considered trying it. Then I saw that there was a wooden trellis on the wall for the climbing fruit, and I thought that it would probably hold me.

I slowly climbed out and carefully put my feet on the slats. They carried me well and when I saw that it was not dangerous, it occurred to me to take the peaches along. I filled up my pockets as well as my hat.

Then I went home and laid the peaches into my box.

In the afternoon, a letter from the teacher arrived that I was not allowed to step foot into the school again.

That made me happy.

CHAPTER 3: MYDEARS

Der Kindlein

Mydears

Unser Religionslehrer heißt Falkenberg.

Our religion teacher is called Falkenberg.

Er ist klein und dick und hat eine goldene Brille auf.

He is small and fat and wears gold-rimmed glasses.

8 Simplicissimus, 1905, #34, p. 399

Wenn er was Heiliges redet, zwickt er die Augen zu und macht seinen Mund spitzig.

When he says something Holy, he squints his eyes and puckers his lips.

Er faltet immer die Hände und ist recht sanft und sagt zu uns: Ihr Kindlein.

He always folds his hands and gets all gentle and says to us: my dears.

Deswegen haben wir ihn den Kindlein geheißen.

That is why we called him Mydears.

Er ist aber gar nicht so sanft. Wenn man ihn ärgert, macht er grüne Augen wie eine Katze und sperrt einen viel länger ein wie unser Klaßprofessor.

But he is not all that gentle. When you anger him, he makes green eyes like a cat and he locks up you much longer than our class teacher.

Der schimpft einen furchtbar und sagt »mistiger Lausbub«, und zu mir hat er einmal gesagt, er haut das größte Loch in die Wand mit meinem Kopf.

That one scolds you terribly and says "dang rascal", and once he told me he would punch the hugest hole into the wall using my head.

Meinen Vater hat er gut gekannt, weil er im Gebirg war und einmal mit ihm auf die Jagd gehen durfte. Ich glaube, er kann mich deswegen gut leiden und läßt es sich bloß nicht merken.

He had known my father well, because he had been in the mountains and was once allowed to go hunting with him. I think he likes me because of that and just does not show it.

Wie mich der Merkel verschuftet hat, daß ich ihm eine hineinge-haut habe, hat er mir zwei Stun-den Arrest gegeben. Aber wie alle fort waren, ist er auf einmal in das Zimmer gekommen und hat zu mir gesagt: »Mach, daß du heimkommst, du Lauskerl, du grober! Sonst wird die Supp kalt.«

When Merkel ratted me out and I smacked him one, he gave me two hours detention. But when they were all gone, he suddenly came into the room and told me: "Off, get yourself home, you ras-cal, you brute! Otherwise the soup gets cold."

Er heißt Gruber.

His name is Gruber.

Aber der Falkenberg schimpft gar nicht.

But Falkenberg does not scold.

Ich habe ihm einmal seinen Rock von hinten mit Kreide angeschmiert. Da haben alle gelacht, und er hat gefragt: »Warum lacht ihr, Kindlein?«

Es hat aber keiner etwas gesagt; da ist er zum Merkel hingegangen und hat gesagt: »Du bist ein gottesfürchtiger Knabe, und ich glaube, daß du die Lüge verabscheust. Sprich offen, was hat es gegeben?«

Und der Merkel hat ihm gezeigt, daß er voll Kreide hinten ist und daß ich es war.

Der Falkenberg ist ganz weiß geworden im Gesicht und ist schnell auf mich hergegangen. Ich habe gemeint, jetzt krieg ich eine hinein, aber er hat sich vor mich hingestellt und hat die Augen zugezwickt.

Dann hat er gesagt: »Armer Verlorener! Ich habe immer Nachsicht gegen dich geübt, aber ein räudiges Schaf darf nicht die ganze Herde anstecken.«

Er ist zum Rektor gegangen, und ich habe sechs Stunden Karzer gekriegt. Der Pedell hat gesagt, ich wäre dimittiert geworden, wenn mir nicht der Gruber so geholfen hätte. Der Falkenberg hat darauf bestanden, daß ich dimittiert werde, weil ich das Priesterkleid beschmutzt habe. Aber

Once I smeared chalk on the back of his coat. Everyone was laughing and he asked: "Why are you laughing, my dears?"

Nobody said anything; so he went to Merkel and said: "You are a god-fearing boy, and I believe that you abhor the lie. Speak openly, what happened?"

And Merkel told him that his back was full of chalk and that I had done it.

Falkenberg turned all white in his face and quickly walked towards me. I thought I was going to get smacked, but he just stood in front of me and pinched his eyes shut.

Then he said: "Poor lost soul! I have always been lenient towards you, but one mangy sheep cannot be allowed to infect the whole herd."

He went to the principal and I got booked for six hours. The

der Gruber hat gesagt, es ist bloß Übermut und er will meiner Mutter schreiben, ob er mir nicht ein paar herunterhauen darf. Dann haben ihm die andern recht gegeben, und der Falkenberg war voll Zorn. Er hat es sich nicht ankennen lassen, sondern er hat das nächstemal in der Klasse zu mir gesagt: »Du hast gesündigt, aber es ist dir verziehen. Vielleicht wird dich Gott in seiner unbeschreiblichen Güte auf den rechten Weg führen.«

janitor said I would have been expelled if Gruber had not intervened on my behalf. Falkenberg had insisted on me getting expelled, because I had soiled a priest's

9 *Simplicissimus, 1905, #34, p. 399*

cloth. But Gruber had said it was just exuberance and he was going to write to my mother for permission to smack me around a bit. Then the others agreed with him and Falkenberg got real angry. He did not show it, but the next time in the classroom he told me: "You have sinned, but you have been forgiven. Perhaps the Lord in his indescribable goodness will lead you on the right path."

Die sechs Stunden habe ich brummen müssen, und der Falkenberg hat mich nicht mehr aufgerufen; er ist immer an mir vorbeigegangen und hat getan, als wenn er mich nicht sieht.

I had to do the six hours, and Falkenberg never called on me again; he always walked past me and pretended not to see me.

Den Fritz hat er auch nicht leiden können, weil er mein bester Freund ist und immer lacht, wenn er »Kindlein« sagt. Er hat ihn schon zweimal deswegen eingesperrt, und da haben wir gesagt, wir müssen dem Kindlein

He could not stand Fritz either, because he was my best friend and always laughs when he says "my dears". For this, he had locked him up twice already, and so we said we had to do something to Mydears. Fritz thought

etwas antun. Der Fritz hat gemeint, wir müssen ihm einen Pulverfrosch in den Katheder legen; aber das geht nicht, weil man es sieht. Dann haben wir ihm Schusterpech auf den Sessel geschmiert. Er hat sich aber die ganze Stunde nicht daraufgesetzt, und dann ist der Schreiblehrer Bogner gekommen und ist hängengeblieben. Das war auch recht, aber für den Kindlein hätte es mich besser gefreut.

Der Fritz wohnt bei dem Malermeister Burkhard und hat ihm eine grüne Ölfarbe genommen, wie der Katheder ist. Die haben wir vor der Religionsstunde geschwind hingestrichen, wo er den Arm auflegt.

Da hat es auf einmal geheißen, der Falkenberg ist krank, und wir haben Geographie dafür. Da ist der Professor Ulrich eingegangen, weil er voll Farbe geworden ist, und er hat den Pedell furchtbar geschimpft, daß er nichts hinschreibt, wenn frisch gestrichen ist.

Der Kindlein ist uns immer ausgekommen, aber wir haben nicht ausgelassen.

Einmal ist er in die Klasse gekommen mit dem Rektor und hat sich auf den Katheder ge-

we should put a jumping cracker into his lectern; but that does not work because you can see it. Then we smeared cobbler's wax on his seat. But he never sat down for the whole hour and then writing teacher Bogner came and got stuck. That was alright too, but it would have given me more pleasure with Mydears.

Fritz lives with master painter Burkhard and took some green oil paint of his that matched the color of the lectern. Before religion class, we quickly applied it where Mydears puts his arm.

Then we were suddenly told that Falkenberg was ill and we would have geography instead. So, Professor Ulrich lost it because he got paint all over himself and he yelled at the janitor for not putting up a warning sign when something is freshly painted.

Mydears always got away from us, but we never gave up.

Once he came to class with the principal and stood at the lectern. Then he said: "My dears, be

stellt. Dann hat er gesagt: »Kindlein, freuet euch! Ich habe eine herrliche Botschaft für euch. Ich habe lange gespart, und jetzt habe ich für unsere geliebte Studienkirche die Statue des heiligen Aloysius gekauft, weil er das Vorbild der studierenden Jugend ist. Er wird von dem Postament zu euch hinunterschauen, und ihr werdet zu ihm hinaufschauen. Das wird euch stärken.«

Dann hat der Rektor gesagt, daß es unbeschreiblich schön ist von dem Falkenberg, daß er die Statue gekauft hat, und daß unser Gymnasium sich freuen muß. Am Samstag kommt der Heilige, und wir müssen ihn abholen, wo die Stadt anfangt, und am Sonntag ist Enthüllungsfeier.

Da sind sie hinausgegangen und haben es in den anderen Klaßzimmern gesagt. Und ich und der Fritz sind miteinander heimgegangen.

Da hat der Fritz gesagt, daß der Kindlein es mit Fleiß getan hat, daß wir den Aloysius am Samstagnachmittag holen müssen, weil er uns nicht gönnt, daß wir frei haben. Ich habe auch geschimpft und habe gesagt, ich möchte, daß der Wagen umschmeißt.

happy! I have a wonderful message for you. I have been saving for a long time and now I have bought a statue of the Holy Aloysius for our beloved school church, because he is the role model for the student youth. He will look down on you from the pedestal and you will look up to him. That will strengthen you."

Then the principal said that it was indescribably nice of Falkenberg that he had bought the statue and that our Gymnasium should rejoice. The Saint would arrive on Saturday and we would have to pick him up at the town limits, and on Sunday there would be the unveiling ceremony.

Then they left and told the other classrooms. And I and Fritz went home together.

Fritz said that Mydears had really done a number on us for having us pick up Aloysius on Saturday afternoon, just because wanted to ruin our day off. I joined the rant and said that I wished the wagon would overturn.

Dem Fritz sein Hausherr hat es schon gewußt, weil es in der Zeitung gestanden ist. Er kann uns gut leiden und redet oft mit uns und schenkt uns eine Zigarre. Auf den Falkenberg hat er einen Zorn, weil er glaubt, daß sein Pepi wegen dem Falkenberg die Prüfung in der Lateinschule nicht bestanden hat. Ich glaube aber, daß der Pepi zu dumm ist.

Fritz's landlord already knew about it, because the newspaper had mentioned it. He likes us well and often chats with us and lets us have a cigar. He holds a grudge against Falkenberg, because he believes that Pepi did not pass the Latin school exam because of Falkenberg. I believe, however, that Pepi is just too dumb.

Der Hausherr hat gelacht, daß soviel in der Zeitung gestanden ist von dem Heiligen. Er hat gesagt, daß er von Gips ist und daß er ihn nicht geschenkt möchte. Er ist von Mühldorf. Da ist er schon lang gestanden, und niemand hat ihn mögen. Vielleicht hat ihn der Steinmetz hergeschenkt, aber der Falkenberg macht sich schön damit und tut, als wenn er viel gekostet hat. Das ist ein scheinheiliger Tropf, hat der Hausherr gesagt, und wir haben auch geschimpft über den Kindlein.

The landlord laughed that the newspaper made so an ado about the Saint. He said that he was made from gypsum and that he would not want him for a present. He is from Mühldorf. There he had been standing for a long time and nobody liked him. Maybe the stonemason had donated him, but Falkenberg makes himself look good and talks as if he had cost a lot. That is a hypocritical twit, the landlord had said, and we also ripped on Mydears.

Dann ist der Samstag gekommen. Das ganze Gymnasium ist aufgestellt worden, und dann haben wir durch die Stadt gehen müssen. Vorne ist der Rektor mit dem Falkenberg gegangen, und dann sind die Professoren gekommen. Der Gruber war nicht dabei, weil er Protestant ist. Oben auf dem Berg ist ein Wirts-

Then Saturday came around. The whole Gymnasium was lined up and we had to walk through the whole town. The principal walked up front with Falkenberg, followed by the professors. Gruber was not part of this, because he was a Protestant. Up on the hill there is a tavern, where the street comes in from Mühldorf. There we stopped and

haus, wo die Straße von Mühldorf herkommt. Da haben wir gehalten und haben gewartet. Eine halbe Stunde haben wir stehen müssen, bis der Pedell dahergelaufen ist und hat geschrien: »Jetzt bringen sie ihn.«

waited. We had to stand for half an hour until the janitor came running and hollered: "Now they're bringing him."

10 "Bäcker Meyer", 1862. http://www.historischer-verein-forstenried.de

Da ist ein Leiterwagen gekommen, da war eine große Kiste darauf. Der Falkenberg ist hingegangen und hat den Fuhrmann gefragt, ob er von Mühldorf ist und den heiligen Aloysius dabei hat.

A rack wagon appeared carrying a large box. Falkenberg approached it and asked the waggoner whether he came from Mühldorf and was bringing the Holy Aloysius along.

11 Leiterwagen – rack wagon

Der Fuhrmann hat gesagt ja, und er hat einen in der Kiste. Da hat sich der Kindlein geärgert, daß der Wagen so schlecht aussieht und keine Tannenbäume darauf sind.

The wagoner said yes and that he had one in the box. Then Mydears got angry, because the wagon was so shabby and did not have any pine trees on top.

Aber der Fuhrmann hat gesagt, das geht ihn nichts an, er tut bloß, was ihm sein Herr anschafft.

But the wagoner said that this was none of his concern, he was just doing as told by his master.

Da haben wir hinter dem Wagen hergehen müssen, und die Glocken von der Studienkirche haben geläutet, bis wir dort waren.

Then we had to march behind the wagon and the bells of the school church were ringing until we arrived there.

Vor der Kirche hat der Fuhrmann gehalten, und er hat die Kiste heruntertun wollen.

The wagoner stopped in front of the church and moved to unload the box.

Aber der Falkenberg hat ihn nicht lassen. Die vier Größten von der Oberklasse mußten sie heruntertun und in die Sakristei tragen. Das war der Pointner und der Reichenberger, die andern zwei habe ich nicht gekannt.

But Falkenberg did not let him. The four tallest senior students had to take it down and carry it into the sacristy. Pointner and Reichenberger were among them, but I did not know the other two.

Wir haben gehen dürfen, und das Läuten hat aufgehört. Bloß die vier Oberklaßler mußten dabei sein, wie der Heilige aufgestellt wurde; die anderen nicht, weil erst morgen die Einweihung war. Wir haben aber gewußt, wo er hingestellt wird. Bei dem dritten Fenster, weil dort das Postament war und Blumen herum. Der Fritz und ich sind heimgegangen; zuerst war der Friedmann Karl dabei. Da hat der Fritz gesagt, er muß noch viel büffeln auf den Montag, weil er die dritte Konjugation noch nicht gelernt hat.

We were allowed to leave and the bell ringing had stopped. Only the four seniors had to be present when the Saint was erected; the others not, because the consecration was not until tomorrow. But we know where he was put. Near the third window, because that is where the pedestal was, surrounded with flowers. Fritz and I went home; at first, Friedmann's Karl was with us. Fritz said that he still had to memorize a lot until Monday, because he had not learned the third conjugation yet.

12 Holy Aloysius, Moriz Schlachter [Public domain], via Wikimedia Commons

»Die haben wir ja gar nicht auf«, hat der Friedmann gesagt.

"That's not even our homework," Friedmann said.

»Freilich haben wir sie aufgekriegt. Der Gruber hat es ganz deutlich gesagt«, hat der Fritz gesagt. Da ist dem Friedmann angst geworden, weil er immer furchtsam ist, und er ist der Erste.

"Of course it is. Gruber said so very clearly," Fritz said. Then Friedmann got worried, because he is always fearful, and he is the top student.

Er ist gleich von uns weggelaufen und der Fritz hat zu mir gesagt: »Jetzt haben wir unsere Ruhe vor ihm.«

He immediately ran off and Fritz told me: "Now he does not bother us anymore."

Ich fragte, warum er ihn fortgeschickt hat, aber der Fritz wartete, bis niemand in der Nähe war. Dann sagte er, daß er jetzt

I asked why he had sent him off, but Fritz waited until nobody was in earshot. Then he said that he knew how we could get

weiß, wie wir den Kindlein daran kriegen, und daß wir auf den Aloysius einen Stein hineinschmeißen.

Ich glaubte zuerst, er macht Spaß, aber es war ihm Ernst, und er sagte, daß er es allein tut, wenn ich nicht mithelfe.

Da habe ich versprochen, daß ich mittue, aber ich habe mich gefürchtet, denn wenn es aufkommt, ist alles hin. Aber der Fritz hat gesagt, dann muß man es so machen, daß kein Mensch nichts merkt, und so eine Gelegenheit kriegen wir nicht mehr, daß wir dem Kindlein etwas antun, was er sich merkt.

Wir haben ausgemacht, daß wir uns um acht Uhr bei den zwei Kastanien an der Salzach treffen. Ich habe daheim gesagt, daß ich mit dem Fritz die dritte Konjugation lernen muß, und bin gleich nach dem Abendessen fort.

Es war schon dunkel, wie ich an die Kastanien hinkam, und ich war froh, daß mir niemand begegnet ist.

Der Fritz war schon da, und wir haben noch gewartet, bis es ganz dunkel war. Dann sind wir neben der Salzach gegangen; einmal haben wir Schritte gehört. Da sind

Mydears and that we should throw a rock at Aloysius.

At first I thought he was kidding, but he was serious and said that he would do it alone if I would not help.

So I promised to go along, but I was scared, because everything would go downhill if this became known. But Fritz said that it had to be done in a way that nobody noticed, and that we would never get an opportunity like this again to do something to Mydears that he would remember.

We agreed to meet at the two chestnut trees by the Salzach at eight o'clock. At home, I said that I had to study the third conjugation with Fritz, and I left right after dinner.

It was getting dark when I reached the two chestnut trees, and I was glad that I had not run into anyone.

Fritz was already there, but we still waited until it was completely dark. Then we walked along the Salzach; suddenly we heard steps. We hid behind a bush.

wir hinter einen Busch gestanden und haben uns versteckt.

Es war der Notar; der geht immer spazieren und macht ein Gedicht in das Wochenblatt.

It was the Notary; he always takes a walk and composes a poem for the weekly paper.

Er hat nichts gemerkt, und wir sind erst wieder vorgegangen, wie er schon weit weg war.

He did not notice anything, and we stepped forward when he was already far away.

Das Gymnasium und die Studienkirche sind am Ende von der Stadt; es ist kein Mensch hinten, wenn es dunkel ist. Bloß der Pedell, aber er ist auch nicht hinten, sondern beim Sternbräu.

The Gymnasium and the school church are at the end of town; when it is dark, there is nobody there. Only the janitor perhaps, but he was in the Sternbräu tavern.

Wir sind hingekommen, und jeder hat einen Stein genommen.

When we arrived, we each picked up a rock.

Wir haben die Fenster noch gesehen. Das dritte war es. Der Fritz sagte zu mir: »Du mußt gut rechts schmeißen; wenn es an die Wand hingeht, prallt es schon hinein. Und du mußt halb so hoch schmeißen, wie das Fenster ist; ich probier es höher, dann erwischt ihn schon einer.« »Es ist schon recht«, sagte ich, und dann haben wir geschmissen. Es hat stark gescheppert, und wir haben gewußt, daß wir das Fenster getroffen haben. Gleich hinter dem Gymnasium sind Haselnußstauden; da haben wir uns versteckt und haben gehorcht. Es ist ganz still gewesen, und der Fritz sagte: »Das ist fein gegangen. Jetzt

We could still make out the windows. It was the third one. Fritz told me: "You have to aim to the right; if it hits the wall, it'll still go in. And you have to throw half as high as the window; I'll try it higher, then one of them will hit him." "Okay," I said, and then we threw. There was a loud crash and we knew that we had hit the window. Right behind the Gymnasium were some hazelnut bushes; there we hid and listened. It was all quiet and Fritz said: "That went nicely. Now we have to watch out that nobody sees us leave."

müssen wir achtgeben, daß uns niemand gehen sieht.«

Wir sind schnell gelaufen, aber wenn wir etwas gehört haben, sind wir stehengeblieben. Es ist uns niemand begegnet, und beim Fritz seinem Hausherrn sind wir hinten über den Gartenzaun gestiegen und ganz still die Stiege hinaufgegangen.

Then we ran quickly, but whenever we heard anything, we stood still. We did not meet anybody and at the house of Fritz's landlord we climbed over the garden fence in back and sneaked up the stairs.

Der Fritz hat sein Licht brennen lassen, daß sie glaubten, er ist daheim. Wir setzten uns an den Tisch und haben uns abgewischt, weil wir so schwitzten.

Fritz had left his light on, so they would think he was home. We set down at the table and wiped us off, because we were sweating so much.

Auf einmal ist wer über die Treppe gegangen und hat geklopft. Ich bin zum Fenster hingelaufen, weil ich noch ganz naß war, aber der Fritz hat seinen Kopf in die Hand gelegt und hat getan, als wenn er lernt.

Suddenly someone came up the stairs and knocked. I ran to the window, because I was still dripping, but Fritz put his head in his hand and pretended to study.

Es war die Magd vom Expeditor Friedmann, und sie hat gesagt, einen schönen Gruß vom Friedmann Karl, und er glaubt nicht, daß wir die dritte Konjugation aufhaben, weil er den Raithel gefragt hat und den Kanzler, und keiner hat etwas gewußt.

It was Expeditor Friedmann's maid, and she brought greetings from Friedmann's Karl, and he did not think that we had to learn the third conjugation, because he had asked Raithel and the Chancellor, and nobody knew anything.

Der Fritz hat seinen Kopf nicht aufheben mögen, weil er auch so geschwitzt hat. Er hat gesagt, daß er es deutlich gehört hat, und er lernt die dritte Konjugation.

Fritz did not want to lift his head, because he was also sweating profusely. He said that he had heard clearly, and that he was learning the third conjugation.

Da ist die Magd gegangen, und wir haben gehört, wie sie drunten zu der Frau Burkhard gesagt hat, daß der Fritz so fleißig lernt und daß es grausam ist, wieviel man in der Schule lernen muß.

So the maid left and we heard her say to Mrs Burkhard downstairs that Fritz was studying with such diligence and that it was cruel how much they had to learn in school.

Am andern Tag ist Sonntag gewesen, und um acht Uhr war die Kirche und die Feier für den Aloysius.

The next day was Sunday, and at eight o'clock was church and the celebration for Aloysius.

Aber sie ist nicht gewesen.

But that did not happen.

Wie ich hingekommen bin, war alles schwarz vor der Türe, so viele Leute sind herumgestanden.

When I arrived, it was all black in front of the door, because so many people were standing around there.

Um den Pedell ist ein großer Kreis gewesen, der Rektor ist daneben gestanden und der Falkenberg auch.

There was a large circle around the janitor, and the Principal stood next to him as well as Falkenberg.

Sie haben geredet und dann haben sie zu dem Fenster hinaufgezeigt. Da waren zwei Löcher darin.

They were talking and then they were pointing up to the window. There were two holes.

Ich habe den Raithel gefragt, was es gibt.

I asked Raithel what was up.

»Dem Aloysius is die Nase weggehaut«, hat er gesagt.

"Aloysius his nose got knocked off," he said.

»Haben s' ihn beim Aufstellen runterfallen lassen?« habe ich gefragt.

"Did they drop him, when they put him up?" I asked.

»Nein, es sind Steine hineingeflogen«, hat er gesagt.

"No, some rocks flew in," he said.

Der Föckerer und der Friedmann und der Kanzler sind hergekommen. Der Föckerer macht sich immer gescheit, und er hat gesagt, daß er es zuerst gehört hat.

Föckerer and Friedmann and the Chancellor came along. Föckerer always likes to appear smart and he said that he had heard it first.

Er ist dabei gewesen, wie der Falkenberg gekommen ist, und der Pedell hat es ihm gezeigt. Da ist ein furchtbarer Spektakel gewesen, denn wie sie die Löcher in dem Fenster gesehen haben, sind sie hineingegangen, und da haben sie gesehen, daß von dem Aloysius seinem Kopf die Nase und der Mund weg waren, und unten ist alles voll Gips gewesen, und dann hat man zwei Steiner gefunden. Der Föckerer hat gesagt, wenn es aufkommt, wer es getan hat, glaubt er, daß man ihn köpft.

He had been there when Falkenberg came, and the janitor had shown it to him. There had been a terrible ruckus, because when they saw the holes in the window, they had gone inside and had seen that Aloysius' nose and mouth were gone, and everything below was full of gypsum, and then they had found two rocks. Föckerer said that when they find the one who did this, they would behead him.

Der Pedell hat es gesagt.

The janitor had said so.

Ich habe mich nicht gerührt, und der Fritz auch nicht. Er hat nur zum Friedmann gesagt, daß er jetzt die dritte Konjugation kann.

I did not move, and neither did Fritz. He only said to Friedmann that he knows the third conjugation now.

Ich bin zu den Großen hingegangen, wo die Professoren gestanden sind. Der Pedell hat immer geredet.

I went over to the seniors where the all professors were standing. The janitor was talking non-stop.

Er erzählte alles immer wieder von vorne.

He told it all over and over again.

Er hat gesagt, daß er daheim war und nachgedacht hat, ob er vielleicht eine Halbe Bier trinken soll. Auf einmal hat seine Frau gesagt, es hat gescheppert, als wenn eine Fensterscheibe hin ist. »Wo soll eine Fensterscheibe hin sein?« hat er gefragt. Dann haben sie gehorcht, und er hat die Haustüre aufgemacht. Da ist ihm gewesen, als wenn er einen Schritt hört, und er ist in sein Zimmer und hat sein Gewehr geholt. Dann ist er heraus und hat dreimal »Wer da?« gerufen. Denn beim Militär hat er es so gelernt, wo er doch ein Feldwebel war. Und im Krieg haben sie es so gemacht, da ist immer einer Posten gestanden, und wenn er etwas Verdächtiges gehört hat, hat er »Wer da?« rufen müssen. Es hat sich aber nichts mehr gerührt, und er ist im Hofe dreimal herumgegangen und hat nichts gesehen. Und dann ist er zum Sternbräu gegangen, weil er gedacht hat, daß er eine Halbe Bier trinken muß. Er hat gesagt, wenn er einen gesehen hätte, dann hätte er geschossen, denn wenn einer keine Antwort nicht gibt auf »Wer da?«, muß er erschossen werden.

He said that he had been home thinking about whether to drink a half beer. Suddenly his wife had said that there was a racket as if a window had been broken. "What window should be broken?" he had asked. Then they had listened and he had opened the front door. He thought he had heard a step and he had gone into his room to fetch his shotgun. Then he had gone outside and called "who there?" three times. Because in the military that is how he had learned it, when he had been a sergeant. And in the war they had done it like this, there had always been a guard and whenever he heard something suspicious, he was to call "who there?". Nothing was stirring then anymore and he had circled the yard three times and had not seen anything. And then he went to Sternbräu, because he had thought that he had to drink a half beer. He said if he had seen anybody he would have shot, because anybody who does not answer to "who there?" must be shot.

Der Rektor hat ihn gefragt, ob er einen Verdacht hat.

The Principal asked him whether he had any suspicion.

Da hat der Pedell gesagt, daß er schon einen hat, aber er hat mit

The janitor said that he did, but he blinked his eyes and said that

den Augen geblinzelt und hat gesagt, daß er es noch nicht sagen darf, weil er ihn sonst nicht erwischt. Wenn nicht gleich so viele Leute herumgestanden wären, hat der Pedell gesagt, dann hätte er ihn vielleicht schon, weil er die Fußspuren gemessen hätte, aber jetzt ist alles verwischt.

he could not tell yet, because otherwise he would not catch him. If there had not been so many people, the janitor said, then he could have already caught him, because he would have measured the footsteps, but now everything was wiped out.

Da hat ihn der Rektor gefragt, ob er glaubt, daß er ihn noch kriegt. Da hat der Pedell wieder mit den Augen geblinzelt und hat gesagt, daß er ihn noch erwischt, weil alle Verbrecher zweimal kommen und den Ort anschauen. Und er paßt jetzt die ganze Nacht mit dem Gewehr und schreit bloß einmal »Wer da?« und er schießt gleich.

Then the Principal asked him whether he believed that he could still catch him. The janitor blinked with his eyes again and said that he would still catch him, because all criminals come back to look at the site. And now he would sit there all night with his gun and call "who there?" only once before he shoots.

Der Falkenberg hat gesagt, er will beten, daß der Verbrecher aufkommt, aber heute ist keine Kirche nicht, weil man den Aloysius wegräumen muß, und wir müssen heimgehen und auch beten, daß es offenbar wird. Da sind alle gegangen, aber ich bin noch stehengeblieben mit dem Friedmann und dem Raithel, weil der Pedell zu uns hergegangen ist und alles wieder erzählt hat, daß es schepperte und daß seine Frau es zuerst gehört hat.

Falkenberg said he wanted to pray that the criminal would be found, but today there would be no church, because they had to put Aloysius away, and we should go home and pray that it would be revealed. So we all left, but I still lingered around with Friedmann and Raithel, because the janitor had walked over to us and told everything again how there had been a racket and his wife had heard it first.

Und er sagte, daß er den Verbrecher erwischt, und bevor eine

And then he said that he would catch the criminal, and before a

Philipp Strazny

Woche ganz vorüber ist, erschießt er ihn, oder er schießt ihm vielleicht auf die Füße.

Ich bin zum Fritz gegangen und habe es erzählt. Da haben wir furchtbar lachen müssen.

Hernach ist eine große Untersuchung gewesen, und in jeder Klasse ist gefragt worden, ob keiner nichts weiß.

Und der Kindlein hat gesagt, daß er seinen Schülern keinen Aloysius nicht mehr schenkt, bevor es nicht aufgekommen ist, wer es getan hat.

Wir haben jetzt vor der Religionsstunde immer ein Gebet sagen müssen zur Entdeckung eines gräßlichen Frevels.

Es hat aber nichts geholfen, und niemand weiß etwas, bloß ich und der Fritz wissen es.

week was over he would shoot him or maybe shoot him in the feet.

I went over to Fritz and told him. Then we had a laughing fit.

Afterwards, there was a big investigation and in every classroom they asked if anybody knew anything.

And Mydears said that he would not give his students another Aloysius anymore until it was determined who had done this.

At the beginning of each religion class now, we had to always say a prayer so that the horrible sacrilege would be discovered.

But nothing helped and nobody knows anything, except for Fritz and me, we know.

CHAPTER 4: GOOD RESOLUTIONS

Gute Vorsätze

Ich war auf einmal furchtbar fromm. Drei Wochen lang hat uns der Religionslehrer Falkenberg vorbereitet auf die heilige Kommunion, und ich habe zum Fritz gesagt: »Wir müssen ein anderes Leben anfangen.«

Den Fritz hat es auch gepackt, weil der Falkenberg einmal so weinte und sagte, er kann es nicht verantworten, einen verdorbenen Knaben zum Tisch des Herrn zu schicken.

Weil neulich vor dem Kommunionsunterricht an die Türschnalle Senf hingeschmiert war und der Religionslehrer meinte, es ist etwas anderes.

Ich habe gewußt, daß es der Fritz getan hat, und ich habe mich schon gefreut, daß der Falkenberg eingegangen ist, aber er hat uns eine halbe Stunde lang beten lassen, daß die Freveltat vorübergeht. Und wie es vorbei

Good Resolutions

I was suddenly terribly pious. For three weeks, Falkenberg, our religion teacher, ha been preparing us for First Holy Communion, and I had said to Fritz: "We have to begin a new life."

Fritz was also convinced, because Falkenberg once started crying and said that he cannot, in good conscience, send a spoilt boy to the Lord's table.

Because recently before First Communion class, some mustard had been smeared on the door handle, and the religion teacher had thought it was something different.

I had known that Fritz had done this, and I was giddy that Falkenberg had fallen for it, but he made us pray for half an hour that the misdeed would disappear. And when we were done,

war, sagte der Fritz zu mir, ob ich glaube, daß wir es weggebetet haben. Ich sagte, daß ich es glaube, weil der Falkenberg sonst nicht aufgehört hätte. Aber ich sagte: »Du mußt auch ein anderer werden, Fritz. Probier es nur, es geht ganz gut.« Er fragte, ob ich es fertiggebracht habe.

Ich sagte: »Ja, weil ich jetzt furchtbar fromm bin. Die Tante Fanny gibt immer Obacht, wenn ich im Gebetbuch lese, und sagt zu Onkel Pepi, daß mit mir eine Veränderung geschehen ist. Sie glaubt, daß ich in mich gegangen bin, und ich glaube es auch, weil ich jetzt schon eine Viertelstunde lang beten kann und nicht denke, wie ich der Tante etwas antue.«

Der Fritz sagte, er will morgen anfangen, aber heute muß er noch dem Schuster Rettenberger das Fenster einschmeißen, denn er hat ihn beim Pedell verschuftet, daß er ihn mit einer Zigarre gesehen hat.

Ich sagte, er soll warten bis nach der Kommunion, weil ich mittun möchte, aber Fritz sagte, daß er nicht beten kann, vor er das Fenster kaputtgeschmissen hat, weil er voll Zorn ist.

Der Rettenberger lacht immer, wenn er ihn sieht, und gestern

Fritz asked me whether I believed that we had prayed it away. And I said that I did believe so, because Falkenberg would not have let us stop otherwise. But I said: "You also must become a different person, Fritz. Just try, and it will be okay." He asked if I had managed to change.

I said: "Yes, because I am terribly pious now. Aunt Fanny always watches me read the prayer book, and she says to Uncle Pepi that there has been a change in me. She believes that I have done some soul-searching, and I believe it too, because now I am able to pray for a whole quarter of an hour without thinking about what I can do to Auntie."

Fritz said that he wanted to begin tomorrow, but that he still had to throw in Shoemaker Rettenberger's window, because he had ratted him out with the janitor after seeing him with a cigar.

I said he should wait until after Communion, because I wanted to be part of it, but Fritz said that he was unable to pray before the window was thrown in, because he was just too irate.

Rettenberger always laughs when he sees him and yesterday

hat er ihm nachgeschrien: »Gelt, ich hab dich schön erwischt, du Lausbub, du miserabliger!«

Da hab ich denn Fritz recht gegeben, weil es eine solche Gemeinheit ist, und ich hätte so gerne mitgetan.

Aber es ging nicht, denn ich habe mich schon acht Tage lang vorbereitet, und da hätte ich wieder von vorne anfangen müssen.

Das ist gar nicht leicht.

Die Tante Fanny hat Obacht gegeben, daß ich nicht auslasse. Sie hat mir recht wenig zum Essen gegeben, weil man sich täglich einmal abtöten muß, aber die Magd hat zu mir gesagt, daß sie ein Knack ist und sparen will.

Vor dem Bettgehen habe ich die Gewissenserforschung treiben müssen; da habe ich den Beichtspiegel vorgelesen, und der Onkel Pepi und die Tante haben alles erklärt. Der Onkel Pepi ist ganz heilig. Er ist Sekretär am Gericht, aber er sagt oft, daß er ein Pfarrer hat werden wollen, aber weil er kein Geld hatte, ist er mit dem Studieren nicht ganz fertig geworden.

he called after him: "See, I got you good, you rascal, you miserable!"

There I had to agree with Fritz, because this was so mean, and I would have really liked to participate.

But there was no way, because I had already been preparing for eight days, and I would have had to start all over again.

That is not so easy.

Aunt Fanny paid attention that I did not skip anything. She gave me very little to eat, because one has to kill oneself a little every day, but the maid told me that she is just a scrooge and wants to save money.

Before bedtime, I had to examine my conscience; for this, I read the Spiritual Exercises aloud and Uncle Pepi and Auntie explained it all to me. Uncle Pepi is all Holy. He is a secretary at the courts of law, but he often says that he would have liked to become a priest, but since he had no money, he never got done with his studies.

13 Simplicissimus, 1909, #1, p. 5

Wie er einmal mit der Tante recht gestritten hat, da hat die Tante gesagt, daß er zu dumm war für das Gymnasium. Der Falkenberg mag ihn gerne, weil er alle Tage in die Kirche geht und ihm alles sagt, was die Leute im Wirtshaus reden.

Meine Mutter hat ihm geschrieben, daß er mich unterstützt und belehrt für die heilige Handlung, damit ich so fromm werde wie er.

Das hat ihn gefreut, und er ist alle Tage bis neun Uhr dageblieben und hat gepredigt. Dann ist er ins Wirtshaus gegangen. Einmal hat er aus einem Buche vorgelesen, daß man täglich sein Gewissen erforschen muß und es machen soll wie der heilige Ignatius.

Once he had quite an argument with Auntie, and Auntie had said that he had been too stupid for Gymnasium. Falkenberg liked him, because he came to church every day and told him everything the people said in the tavern.

My mother had asked him in a letter to support me and instruct me in Holy activities, so that I would become as pious as he was.

That had made him happy, and every day he stayed until nine o'clock and preached. Then he went to the tavern. Once he read from a book that one should examine one's conscience daily and to do it like the Holy Ignatius.

Er hatte alle Sünden in ein Büchlein geschrieben und es unter sein Kopfkissen gesteckt.

Das habe ich auch getan; aber da habe ich es vergessen, und wie ich aus der Klasse heimkam, hat mich der Onkel Pepi gerufen und gesagt: »Du hast voriges Jahr aus meiner Hosentasche zwei Mark gestohlen.« Da habe ich gemerkt, daß er meine Gewissenserforschung gelesen hat, aber es waren bloß sechzig Pfennig.

Die Tante hat gesagt, weil es ein Beichtgeheimnis ist, darf man es meiner Mutter nicht schreiben.

Da war ich froh. Nach dem Essen hat der Onkel das Seelenbad vorgelesen, wo eine Geschichte darin stand vom heiligen Antonius. Zu dem ist ein Mann gekommen, der viele Sünden hatte, und hat beichten wollen. Der Heilige hat ihm angeschafft, daß er seine Sünden aufschreibt, und das tat der Mann.

Wie er dann seine Sünden gelesen hat, ist jedesmal eine Sünde ausgelöscht worden.

Der Onkel hat die Geschichte zweimal vorgelesen, und dann hat er zur Tante gesagt: »Liebe Fanny, es ist auch für uns eine Lehre in diesem wunderbaren

He had put all sins into a booklet and stuffed it under his pillow.

I did that too, but then I forgot about it and when I came home from class, Uncle Pepi called me over and said: "Last year you stole two Marks out of my pant pockets." That tipped me off that he had been reading my examinations of conscience, although it had only been 60 pennies.

The aunt had said that it was a confessional secret, so one was not allowed to write about this to my mother.

I was glad. After dinner, Uncle read from the Soul Bath, which had a story about the Holy Antonius. A man had come to him who had committed many sins, and he had wanted to confess. The Saint had told him to write down his sins, and the man had done so.

And each time he had read his sins, one sin was expunged.

The uncle read the story twice, and then he said to the Aunt: "Dear Fanny, this wonderful event has something to teach us

Vorfalle. Wenn Gott die Sünden verzeiht, müssen wir dem Beispiele folgen.«

»Aber seine Mutter muß es ersetzen«, sagte die Tante.

»Natürlich«, sagte der Onkel, »das ist notwendig wegen der Gerechtigkeit.«

»Und du sollst nicht so viel Geld in den Hosensack stecken«, sagte die Tante. »Warum nimmst du so viel Geld in das Wirtshaus mit? Drei Glas Bier sind genug für dich, das macht sechsunddreißig Pfennig; aber natürlich, ihr müßt ja der Kellnerin ein Trinkgeld geben, als wenn du etwas zum Verschenken hättest mit deinem Gehalt.«

»Das gehört nicht hierher«, sagte der Onkel; »was soll der Bursche denken, wenn du seine Aufmerksamkeit ablenkst.«

»Er wird denken, daß er dir noch mehr stiehlt, wenn du so viel Geld in den Hosensack steckst«, sagte die Tante. »Wer weiß, wieviel er schon genommen hat. Du natürlich weißt es nicht, weil du ja nicht achtgibst, als hättest du das Gehalt von einem Präsidenten.«

»Ich habe bloß einmal die sechzig Pfennig genommen«, sagte ich.

as well. If God forgives the sins, we have to follow this example."

"But his mother has to replace it," said the Aunt.

"Of course," said the Uncle, "justice requires it."

"And you should not stick that much money into your pant pockets," said the Aunt. "Why do you take that much money to the tavern? Three glasses of beer are enough for you, that's thirty-six pennies; but, of course, you have to tip the waitress, as if you had money to give away on your salary."

"This is not the time," said the Uncle, "what should the lad think if you divert his attention."

"He will think that he is going to steal more from you if you put that much money into your pant pockets," said the Aunt. "Who knows how much he has already taken. You certainly do not know, because you do not pay attention, as if you had the salary of a president."

"I only took sixty pennies that one time," I said.

»Es waren wenigstens zwei Mark«, sagte der Onkel, »aber ich verzeihe dir, wenn du es aufrichtig bereust und gegen diesen Fehler ankämpfen willst. Du mußt den heiligen Vorsatz fassen, daß du es nie mehr tust und die Versuchung meidest und meinen Hosensack nie mehr aussuchst.«

Ich war furchtbar zornig, aber ich durfte es nicht merken lassen. Ich dachte, wenn die Kommunion vorbei ist, dann will ich ihn schon ärgern, daß er blau wird. Vielleicht mache ich seine Goldfische kaputt oder etwas anderes.

Es waren bloß mehr fünf Tage.

Der Tante Frieda ihre Anna durfte heuer auch zum erstenmal zur Kommunion gehen, und sie haben ein ekelhaftes Getue mit ihr. Die Anna ist eine falsche Katze, und ich habe sie nie leiden mögen, aber jetzt bin ich noch giftiger auf sie, weil die Tante Frieda immer von ihr redet und sich so dick macht damit.

Die Tante Frieda ist die beste Freundin von der Tante Fanny, und sie sagen allemal etwas über meine Mutter, wenn sie beisammen sind.

Am Abend ist die Tante Frieda öfter gekommen, und wie sie

"It was at least two Marks," said the Uncle, "but I forgive you if you sincerely regret it and want to combat your fault. You have to make a Holy resolution to never do it again and to avoid the temptation and never search my pant pockets ever again."

I was terribly angry, but I could not let it be known. I thought that when Communion is over, then I would aggravate him until he turns blue. Maybe I would destroy his goldfish or something else.

Only five more days.

Aunt Frieda's Anna was allowed to go to Communion for the first time today, and they made a disgusting fuss about her. Anna is a deceitful cat, and I had never liked her, but now I felt even more viperous against her, because Aunt Frieda talks about her incessantly and brags about it so much.

Aunt Frieda is best friends with Aunt Fanny, and they always talk about my mother when they are together.

In the evenings, Aunt Frieda often came over, and once, when

einmal gehört hat, daß wir An- she heard that we were perform-
dachtsübung machen, hat sie ing devotional exercises, she said
zum Onkel Pepi gesagt: to Uncle Pepi:

»Du tust ein gutes Werk an dem "You are doing good work with
Burschen; ich fürchte bloß daß the lad; I only fear that it won't
es nicht viel hilft.« be of much help."

Und dann fragte sie mich, ob ich And then she asked me whether
mich auf die heilige Handlung I was properly preparing for the
ordentlich vorbereite. sacred occasion.

Ich sagte, daß ich mich schon I said that I had been preparing
zwei Wochen vorbereite. for two weeks already.

»Vorbereiten und vorbereiten ist "There is a difference between
ein Unterschied. Ach Gott«, preparing and preparing. Oh,
sagte sie, »ich weiß nicht, mein God," she said, "I don't know,
Ännchen flößt mir beinahe my Annie almost scares me. She
Angst ein. So durchgeistigt seems so spirited through and
kommt sie mir vor und so ange- through and so enraptured with
griffen von dem Gedanken an the thought of her First Com-
ihre erste Kommunion. Und munion. And just imagine what
denkt euch nur, wie das Kind the child says! Last Friday, I
spricht! Am letzten Freitag wanted to give her a little bit of
wollte ich ihr ein bißchen meat soup, because she is so del-
Fleischsuppe geben, weil sie icate. But she did not want to
doch so schwächlich ist. Aber sie have it for anything in the world.
hat es um keinen Preis nicht ge- I said it was just a trifle. 'No', she
nommen. Ich sagte, es ist doch said, 'dear Mother, can be a trifle
eine Kleinigkeit. 'Nein', sagte sie, what insults God?' And her eyes
'liebe Mutter, kann das eine Klei- were glistening. I got all queasy.
nigkeit sein, was Gott beleidigt?' Dear Mother, she had said, can
Und ihre Augen glänzten ganz be a trifle what insults God?"
dabei. Mir ist ganz anders gewor-
den. Liebe Mutter, hat sie gesagt,
kann das eine Kleinigkeit sein,
was Gott beleidigt?«

Tante Fanny war erstaunt und Aunt Fanny was surprised and
nickte mit dem Kopfe auf und nodded her head up and down,

and Uncle Pepi made big eyes at me and they were all watery. He said to me: "Do you hear that?"

I said that I had already read this, because it was a Saint story from our prep book.

Aunt Frieda was furious because I knew this. She said that she did not believe it, because I was always lying, but even if it was true, it did not matter, because one could see that Annie had taken the moral to heart.

And she told how Anna had not been able to fall asleep yesterday and had been sitting in bed crying. "What is the matter, child?" she had asked. "I ate a piece of bread rind," Anna had said. "Why should you not eat no bread rind?" Aunt Frieda had asked. "Because supper was done and the bread rind was not meant for me anymore, tt was not right and I had been so resolved not to commit any more sins," Anna had said, and then she had cried even more. "That's how the child is," Aunt Frieda said, "sometimes she seems otherworldly to me, and I cannot console her."

»Es gibt Kinder, welche zwei und drei Mark aus einem Hosensacke stehlen und keine Unruhe verspüren«, sagte Onkel Pepi.

"There are children who steal two or three Marks from some pant pockets and do not feel uneasy at all," Uncle Pepi said.

Und Tante Frieda wußte es schon von der Tante Fanny und sagte: »Es ist der Fluch der milden Erziehung.«

And Aunt Frieda already knew about it from Aunt Fanny and said: "That is the curse of a mild upbringing."

Das habe ich alles hören müssen, und ich war froh, wie der Kommunionstag da war. Meine liebe Mutter hat mir einen schwarzen Anzug geschickt und eine große Kerze.

I had to listen to all that and I was glad when the day of Communion came around. My dear mother had sent me a black suit and a large candle.

Sie hat mir geschrieben, daß es ihr weh tut, weil sie nicht dabei sein kann, aber ich soll mir vornehmen, ein anderes Leben anzufangen und ihr bloß Freude zu machen.

She had written to me that she felt bad for not being here, but that I should resolve to begin a different life and to bring joy to her.

Das habe ich mir auch vorgenommen.

I resolved to do so.

Wir waren vierzehn Erstkommunikanten von der Lateinschule, und die Frau Pedell hat zu uns gesagt, daß sie weinen muß, weil wir so feierlich ausgesehen haben, wie lauter Engel. Der Fritz hat auch ein ernstes Gesicht gemacht, und ich habe ihn beinahe nicht gekannt, wie er langsam neben mir hergegangen ist.

We were fourteen first communicants from the Latin school and Mrs Janitor had told us that she had tears in her eyes because we looked so festive, like a bunch of angels. Fritz also made a serious face, and I almost did not recognize him as he was slowly walking next to me.

Wir waren auf der einen Seite aufgestellt. Auf der anderen Seite waren die Mädel aufgestellt von

We were put in a row on one side. On the other side, they put the girls from the girls' school.

der höheren Töchterschule. Da war die Anna dabei. Sie hat ein weißes Kleid angehabt und Locken gebrennt. Ich habe sie in der Sakristei angeredet, bevor wir in die Kirche hineinzogen.

Sie sagte, daß sie heute recht heiß und innig für meine Besserung beten will.

Ich habe mich nicht geärgert, weil ich so friedfertig war, und in der Kirche war ich nicht wie sonst. Ich habe gar nicht gemerkt, daß es lang gedauert hat, und ich habe nicht gedacht, was ich nachher tue. Ich habe gemeint, es ist jetzt alles anders.

Viele Eltern, die da waren, haben ihre Kinder geküßt, wie alles vorbei war, und ich bin zur Tante Fanny und zum Onkel Pepi hingegangen.

Da stand die Tante Frieda bei ihnen und sagte zu mir: »Du hast die dickste Kerze gehabt. Keiner hat eine so dicke Kerze gehabt wie du. Sie hat gewiß um zwei Mark mehr gekostet als die, welche ich meinem Ännchen gab. Aber deine Mutter will immer oben hinaus.«

Und die Tante Fanny sagte: »Natürlich, wenn man einen höheren Beamten geheiratet hat.«

Da habe ich gesehen, daß sie einen nicht fromm sein lassen, und

Anna was with them. She was wearing a white dress and curly locks. I had talked to her in the sacristy before we had proceeded into the church.

She said that she wanted to pray for my betterment with special fervor today.

I did not get angry, because I was so peaceful, and inside the church I was a different person. I did not even notice that it took a long time and I did not spend a thought on what I would do afterwards. I thought everything was different now.

Many parents who were there were kissing their children when everything was over, and I went over to Aunt Fanny and Uncle Pepi.

Aunt Frieda was standing with them and told me: "You had the biggest candle. Nobody had a candle as big as yours. It sure cost at least two Marks more than the one I gave to my Annie. But your mother always has higher aspirations."

And Aunt Fanny said: "Of course, if one is married to someone in a higher office."

That made me realize that they do not let someone be pious, and

ich habe mit dem Fritz was ausgemacht.

Er wohnt auch in der weiten Gasse und kann der Tante Frieda in die Wohnung sehen. Da steht ein Schrank mit einem Spiegel; und der Fritz hat eine Luft Pistole.

Aber jetzt hat der Spiegel auf einmal ein Loch gehabt.

I made some arrangements with Fritz.

He also lives in the wide alley, and he can see into Aunt Frieda's apartment. There is a wardrobe with a mirror; and Fritz had an air pistol.

But now the mirror had suddenly sprung a hole.

CHAPTER 5: BETTERMENT

Besserung

Wie ich in die Ostervakanz gefahren bin, hat die Tante Fanny
gesagt: »Vielleicht kommen wir
zum Besuch zu deiner Mutter.
Sie hat uns so dringend eingeladen, daß wir sie nicht beleidigen
dürfen.«

Und Onkel Pepi sagte, er weiß es
nicht, ob es geht, weil er soviel
Arbeit hat, aber er sieht es ein,
daß er den Besuch nicht mehr
hinausschieben darf. Ich fragte
ihn, ob er nicht lieber im Sommer kommen will, jetzt ist es
noch so kalt, und man weiß
nicht, ob es nicht auf einmal
schneit. Aber die Tante sagte:
»Nein, deine Mutter muß bös
werden, wir haben es schon so
oft versprochen.« Ich weiß aber
schon, warum sie kommen wollen; weil wir auf Ostern das Ge-
räucherte haben und Eier und
Kaffeekuchen, und Onkel Pepi
ißt so furchtbar viel. Daheim
darf er nicht so, weil Tante

Betterment

When I left for the Easter vacation, Aunt Fanny said: "Maybe
we come to visit your mother.
She has invited us so urgently
that we must not insult her."

And Uncle Pepi said that he does
not know whether it will work
out, because he has so much
work, but that he understands
that the visit cannot be post-
poned any further. I asked him
whether he would not prefer to
come in summer, as it is still so
cold now and nobody knows
whether it might not start snow-
ing suddenly. But the Aunt said:
"No, your mother must be getting angry, we have already
promised so many times." But I
already know why they want to
come; because at Easter, we have
smoked food and eggs and coffee cake, and Uncle Pepi eats
such incredible amounts. At

Fanny gleich sagt, ob er nicht an sein Kind denkt.

home he is not allowed to, because Aunt Fanny immediately asks him whether he does not think about his child.

Sie haben mich an den Postomnibus begleitet, und Onkel Pepi hat freundlich getan und hat gesagt, es ist auch gut für mich, wenn er kommt, daß er den Aufruhr beschwichtigen kann über mein Zeugnis.

They accompanied me to the mail omnibus, and Uncle Pepi acted all friendly and said that it would be good for him to come, because he could calm the furor over my report card.

Es ist wahr, daß es furchtbar schlecht gewesen ist, aber ich finde schon etwas zum Ausreden. Dazu brauche ich ihn nicht.

It was truly horribly bad, but I would be able to think up some excuse. I do not need him for that.

Ich habe mich geärgert, daß sie mich begleitet haben, weil ich mir Zigarren kaufen wollte für die Heimreise, und jetzt konnte ich nicht. Der Fritz war aber im Omnibus und hat zu mir gesagt, daß er genug hat, und wenn es nicht reicht, können wir im Bahnhof in Mühldorf noch Zigarren kaufen.

I was angry that they had come along, because I had wanted to buy cigars for the trip home, and now I was not able to. Fritz was on the omnibus and told me that he had enough, and if not, we could still buy cigars at the Mühldorf train station.

Im Omnibus haben wir nicht rauchen dürfen, weil der Oberamtsrichter Zirngiebl mit seinem Heinrich darin war, und wir haben gewußt, daß er ein Freund vom Rektor ist und ihm alles verschuftet.

We were not allowed to smoke on the omnibus, because district judge Zirngiebl was in it with his Heinrich, and we knew that he was friends with the principal and always told him everything.

Bundesarchiv, Bild 146-1973-030C-18
Foto: o.Ang. | o.Dat.

14 Omnibus – horse bus

Der Heinrich hat ihm gleich gesagt, wer wir sind. Er hat es ihm in das Ohr gewispert, und ich habe gehört, wie er bei meinem Namen gesagt hat: »Er ist der Letzte in unserer Klasse und hat in der Religion auch einen Vierer.«

Heinrich immediately told him who we were. He whispered it into his ear and I could hear how he mentioned with my name: "He is the last in our class and even got a D in religion."

Da hat mich der Oberamtsrichter angeschaut, als wenn ich aus einer Menagerie bin, und auf einmal hat er zu mir und zum Fritz gesagt:

Then the district judge looked me over as if I was part of a menagerie, and suddenly he said to me and Fritz:

»Nun, ihr Jungens, gebt mir einmal eure Zeugnisse, daß ich sie mit dem Heinrich dem seinigen vergleichen kann.«

"Now, you boys, hand me your report cards for once, so I can compare them to Heinrich's."

Ich sagte, daß ich es im Koffer habe, und er liegt auf dem Dache vom Omnibus. Da hat er gelacht und hat gesagt, er kennt das schon. Ein gutes Zeugnis hat man immer in der Tasche. Alle Leute im Omnibus haben gelacht, und ich und der Fritz haben uns furchtbar geärgert, bis wir in Mühldorf ausgestiegen sind.

Der Fritz sagte, es reut ihn, daß er nicht gesagt hat, bloß die Handwerksburschen müssen dem Gendarm ihr Zeugnis hergeben. Aber es war schon zu spät. Wir haben im Bahnhof Bier getrunken, da sind wir wieder lustig geworden und sind in die Eisenbahn eingestiegen.

I said that I had mine in the suitcase, and it was on the roof of the omnibus. There he laughed and said he knew about that. A good report card is one you keep in your pocket. All people in the omnibus started laughing and I and Fritz were fuming until we got off in Mühldorf.

Fritz said he regretted not having said that only journeymen had to show their report card to the gendarme. But it was already too late. We had some beer at the train station, which made us cheer up, and we entered the train.

15 train ca. 1900, http://deutschland-um-1900.de.tl/Wirtschaft.htm

Wir haben vom Kondukteur ein Rauchcoupe verlangt und sind in eins gekommen, wo schon Leute darin waren. Ein dicker Mann ist am Fenster gesessen, und an seiner Uhrkette war ein großes silbernes Pferd.

Wenn er gehustet hat, ist das Pferd auf seinem Bauch getanzt und hat gescheppert. Auf der anderen Bank ist ein kleiner Mann gesessen mit einer Brille, und er hat immer zu dem Dicken gesagt, Herr Landrat, und der Dicke hat zu ihm gesagt, Herr Lehrer. Wir haben es aber auch so gemerkt, daß er ein Lehrer ist, weil er seine Haare nicht geschnitten gehabt hat.

We asked the conductor for a smoking compartment and were taken to one which already had some people. A fat man was sitting by the window, and a large silver horse was dangling from his clock chain.

Whenever he coughed, the horse danced and clanked around on his tummy. On the other bench sat a small man with glasses, and he always called the fat one Mr County Commissioner and the fat one called him Mr Teacher. But we had realized anyway that he was a teacher, because he had not cut his hair.

Wie der Zug gegangen ist, hat der Fritz eine Zigarre angezündet und den Rauch auf die Decke geblasen, und ich habe es auch so gemacht.

When the train started moving, Fritz lit a cigar and blew the smoke to the ceiling, and I did the same.

Eine Frau ist neben mir gewesen, die ist weggerückt und hat mich angeschaut, und in der anderen Abteilung sind die Leute aufgestanden und haben herübergeschaut. Wir haben uns furchtbar gefreut, daß sie alle so erstaunt sind, und der Fritz hat recht laut gesagt, er muß sich von dieser Zigarre fünf Kisten bestellen, weil sie so gut ist.

A woman who was sitting next to me moved away and looked at me, and people in the other compartment stood up and looked over. We were thrilled that everybody was so surprised, and Fritz said quite loudly that he wanted to order five boxes of these cigars because they were so good.

Da sagte der dicke Mann: »Bravo, so wachst die Jugend her«, und der Lehrer sagte: »Es ist kein Wunder, was man lesen muß, wenn man die verrohte Jugend sieht.«

Then the fat man said: "Bravo, this is how the youth grows up," and the teacher said: "It is no surprise what you have to read when you see this degenerated youth."

Wir haben getan, als wenn es uns nichts angeht, und die Frau ist immer weitergerückt, weil ich so viel ausgespuckt habe. Der Lehrer hat so giftig geschaut, daß wir uns haben ärgern müssen, und der Fritz sagte, ob ich weiß, woher es kommt, daß die Schüler in der ersten Lateinklasse so schlechte Fortschritte machen, und er glaubt, daß die Volksschulen immer schlechter werden. Da hat der Lehrer furchtbar gehustet, und der Dicke hat gesagt, ob es heute kein Mittel

We acted as if this did not concern us, and the woman kept moving further away, because I was spitting so much. The teacher stared at us with such hostility that we had to get angry, and Fritz asked whether I knew why students in the first class of Latin school made such poor progress, and he believed that the common schools kept getting worse. On that, the teacher started to cough terribly, and the fat one asked whether there was no measure against impertinent

mehr gibt für freche Lausbuben. Der Lehrer sagte, man darf es nicht mehr anwenden wegen der falschen Humanität, und weil man gestraft wird, wenn man einen bloß ein bißchen auf den Kopf haut.

Alle Leute im Wagen haben gebrummt: »Das ist wahr«, und die Frau neben mir hat gesagt, daß die Eltern dankbar sein müssen, wenn man solchen Burschen ihr Sitzleder verhaut. Und da haben wieder alle gebrummt, und ein großer Mann in der anderen Abteilung ist aufgestanden und hat mit einem tiefen Baß gesagt: »Leider, leider gibt es keine vernünftigen Öltern nicht mehr.«

Der Fritz hat sich gar nichts daraus gemacht und hat mich mit dem Fuß gestoßen, daß ich auch lustig sein soll. Er hat einen blauen Zwicker aus der Tasche genommen und hat ihn aufgesetzt und hat alle Leute angeschaut und hat den Rauch durch die Nase gehen lassen.

Bei der nächsten Station haben wir uns Bier gekauft, und wir haben es schnell ausgetrunken. Dann haben wir die Gläser zum Fenster hinausgeschmissen, ob wir vielleicht einen Bahnwärter treffen.

rascals any more. The teacher said that one was not allowed to use it anymore because of this false humanity and that one would be punished even for little slaps on the head.

All people in the wagon grumbled: "That is true," and the woman next to me said that parents should be thankful if such lads would get a spanking on the seat of their pants. Then everybody grumbled again and a tall man in the other section stood up and said with a deep bass: "Unfortunately, there are no judicious parents no more."

Fritz did not mind this at all and bumped me with his foot to make me laugh as well. He pulled a blue pince-nez from his pocket, put it on, and he looked at all the people while he let smoke blow through his nose.

At the next station, we bought some beer and emptied it quickly. Then we threw the glasses out of the window, hoping to hit the station master.

Da schrie der große Mann: »Diese Burschen muß man züchtigen«, und der Lehrer schrie: »Ruhe, sonst bekommt ihr ein paar Ohrfeigen!« Der Fritz sagte: »Sie können's schon probieren, wenn Sie einen Schneid haben.« Da hat sich der Lehrer nicht getraut, und er hat gesagt: »Man darf keinen mehr auf den Kopf hauen, sonst wird man selbst gestraft.« Und der große Mann sagte: »Lassen Sie es gehen, ich werde diese Burschen schon kriegen.« Er hat das Fenster aufgemacht und hat gebrüllt: »Konduktör, Konduktör!«

Then the tall man shouted: "Someone has to discipline these ruffians," and the teacher screamed: "Quiet, or you'll get smacked!" Fritz said: "You are welcome to try if you have the courage." The teacher did not dare, and he said: "One cannot hit anyone on the head any more, otherwise one gets punished oneself." And the tall man said: "Let it go, I will get those guys." He opened the window and shouted: "Conductor, conductor!"

16 *Kondukteur - conductor*

Der Zug hat gerade gehalten, und der Kondukteur ist gelaufen,

The train had just stopped and the conductor came running as if

als wenn es brennt. Er fragte, was es gibt, und der große Mann sagte: »Die Burschen haben Biergläser zum Fenster hinausgeworfen. Sie müssen arretiert werden.«

Aber der Kondukteur war zornig, weil er gemeint hat, es ist ein Unglück geschehen, und es war gar nichts.

Er sagte zu dem Mann: »Deswegen brauchen Sie doch keinen solchen Spektakel nicht zu machen.« Und zu uns hat er gesagt: »Sie dürfen es nicht tun, meine Herren.« Das hat mich gefreut, und ich sagte: »Entschuldigen Sie, Herr Oberkondukteur, wir haben nicht gewußt, wo wir die Gläser hinstellen müssen, aber wir schmeißen jetzt kein Glas nicht mehr hinaus.« Der Fritz fragte ihn, ob er keine Zigarre nicht will, aber er sagte, nein, weil er keine so starken nicht raucht.

Dann ist er wieder gegangen, und der große Mann hat sich hingesetzt und hat gesagt, er glaubt, der Kondukteur ist ein Preuße. Alle Leute haben wieder gebrummt, und der Lehrer sagte immer: »Herr Landrat, ich muß mich furchtbar zurückhalten, aber man darf keinen mehr auf den Kopf hauen.«

there was a fire. He asked what was up and the tall man said: "These guys have tossed beer glasses out the window. They have to get arrested."

But the conductor was furious because he thought there had been some accident and it turned out to be nothing.

He said to the man: "For that you do not need to make no such commotion." And he said to us: "You are not allowed to do this, gentlemen." That made me happy and I said: "Excuse us, Mr Chief Conductor, but we did not know where to put the glasses, but we are not going to throw no more glasses out." Fritz asked him whether he would like a cigar, but he said no, because he did not smoke such strong ones.

Then he left again and the tall man sat down and said he believed the conductor had to be a Prussian. All people were grumbling again and the teacher kept saying: "Mr County Commissioner, I have to really restrain myself, but it is not allowed anymore to hit someone over the head."

Wir sind weitergefahren, und bei der nächsten Station haben wir uns wieder ein Bier gekauft. Wie ich es ausgetrunken habe, ist mir ganz schwindlig geworden, und es hat sich alles zu drehen angefangen. Ich habe den Kopf zum Fenster hinausgehalten, ob es mir nicht besser wird. Aber es ist mir nicht besser geworden, und ich habe mich stark zusammengenommen, weil ich glaubte, die Leute meinen sonst, ich kann das Rauchen nicht vertragen.

We drove on and at the next station we bought another beer. When I had finished, I got all dizzy and everything started spinning. I stuck my head out the window to see if I would feel better. But I did not get better and I tried to hold myself together, because I thought that people would otherwise think that I could not handle smoking.

Es hat nichts mehr geholfen, und da habe ich geschwind meinen Hut genommen.

It was of no use anymore and I quickly grabbed my hat.

Die Frau ist aufgesprungen und hat geschrien, und alle Leute sind aufgestanden, und der Lehrer sagte: »Da haben wir es.« Und der große Mann sagte in der anderen Abteilung: »Das sind die Burschen, aus denen man die Anarchisten macht.«

The woman jumped up and screamed, and all people got up and the teacher said: "There we have it." And the tall man from the other section said. "Those are the guys that eventually get turned into anarchists."

Mir ist alles gleich gewesen, weil mir so schlecht war.

I did not care about any of this, because I was feeling so nauseous.

Ich dachte, wenn ich wieder gesund werde, will ich nie mehr Zigarren rauchen und immer folgen und meiner lieben Mutter keinen Verdruß nicht mehr machen. Ich dachte, wieviel schöner möchte es sein, wenn es mir jetzt nicht schlecht wäre, und ich hätte ein gutes Zeugnis in der

I thought when I get better I would never smoke a cigar again and I would always listen and not cause any more trouble for my dear mother. I thought how much nicer it would be if I were not nauseous, if I had a good report card in my pocket instead of

Tasche, als daß ich jetzt den Hut in der Hand habe, wo ich mich hineingebrochen habe.

a hat in my hand into which I had thrown up.

Fritz sagte, er glaubt, daß es mir von einer Wurst schlecht geworden ist.

Fritz said he believed that I got sick from some bad sausage.

Er wollte mir helfen, daß die Leute glauben, ich bin ein Gewohnheitsraucher.

He was trying to help me by making people think I was a habitual smoker.

Aber es war mir nicht recht, daß er gelogen hat.

But it did not sit right with me that he was lying.

Ich war auf einmal ein braver Sohn und hatte einen Abscheu gegen die Lüge.

Suddenly, I had become a well-behaved son full of contempt against lies.

Ich versprach dem lieben Gott, daß ich keine Sünde nicht mehr tun wollte, wenn er mich wieder gesund werden läßt. Die Frau neben mir hat nicht gewußt, daß ich mich bessern will, und sie hat immer geschrien, wie lange sie den Gestank noch aushalten muß.

I promised the dear Lord that I would not sin ever again if he only let me get healthy. The woman next to me did not know that I wanted to better myself, and she kept screaming how long she was supposed to put up with the stench.

Da hat der Fritz den Hut aus meiner Hand genommen und hat ihn zum Fenster hinausgehalten und hat ihn ausgeleert. Es ist aber viel auf das Trittbrett gefallen, daß es geplatscht hat, und wie der Zug in der Station gehalten hat, ist der Expeditor hergelaufen und hat geschrien: »Wer ist die Sau gewesen? Herrgottsakrament, Konduktör, was ist das für ein Saustall?«

So Fritz took the hat from my hand and held it out the window to empty it. But a lot of it fell on the foot board with a splash, and when the train stopped in the station, the expediter came running and yelled: "Who was this pig? Goddammit, Conductor, what kind of a pig sty is this here?"

Alle Leute sind an die Fenster gestürzt und haben hingeschaut, wo das schmutzige Trittbrett gewesen ist. Und der Kondukteur ist gekommen und hat es angeschaut und hat gebrüllt: »Wer war die Sau?«

Der große Herr sagte zu ihm: »Es ist der nämliche, der mit Bierflaschen schmeißt, und Sie haben es ihm erlaubt.«

»Was ist das mit den Bierflaschen?« fragte der Expeditor.

»Sie sind ein gemeiner Mensch«, sagte der Kondukteur, »wenn Sie sagen, daß ich es erlaubt habe, daß er mit die Bierflaschen schmeißt.«

»Was bin ich?« fragte der große Herr.

»Sie sind ein gemeiner Lügner«, sagte der Kondukteur, »ich habe es nicht erlaubt.«

»Tun Sie nicht so schimpfen«, sagte der Expeditor, »wir müssen es mit Ruhe abmachen.«

Alle Leute im Wagen haben durcheinandergeschrien, daß wir solche Lausbuben sind und daß man uns arretieren muß. Am lautesten hat der Lehrer gebrüllt, und er hat immer gesagt, er ist selbst ein Schulmann. Ich habe nichts sagen können, weil mir so

All the people scrambled to the windows and looked at the dirty foot board. And the conductor came to look at it and screamed: "Who was this pig?"

The tall man said to him: "It is the same one who throws with beer bottles, and you have allowed him to do so."

"What is this business with the beer bottles?" asked the expediter.

"You are a base person," said the conductor, "if you say that I allowed that he throws with beer bottles."

"What am I?" asked the tall gentleman.

"You are a base liar," said the conductor, "I did not allow this."

"Now stop this yelling," said the expediter, "we have to settle this with calm."

All people in the wagon yelled at the same time, that we were such rascals and that we should be arrested. The teacher screamed the loudest, and he kept saying that he is a school man himself. I was not able to say anything because I was feeling so sick, but Fritz

schlecht war, aber der Fritz hat für mich geredet, und er hat den Expeditor gefragt, ob man arretiert werden muß, wenn man auf einem Bahnhof eine giftige Wurst kriegt. Zuletzt hat der Expeditor gesagt, daß ich nicht arretiert werde, aber daß das Trittbrett gereinigt wird, und ich muß es bezahlen. Es kostet eine Mark. Dann ist der Zug wieder gefahren, und ich habe immer den Kopf zum Fenster hinausgehalten, daß es mir besser wird.

In Endorf ist der Fritz ausgestiegen, und dann ist meine Station gekommen. Meine Mutter und Ännchen waren auf dem Bahnhof und haben mich erwartet.

Es ist mir noch immer ein bißchen schlecht gewesen, und ich habe so Kopfweh gehabt.

Da war ich froh, daß es schon Nacht war, weil man nicht gesehen hat, wie ich blaß bin. Meine Mutter hat mir einen Kuß gegeben und hat gleich gefragt: »Nach was riechst du, Ludwig?« Und Ännchen fragte: »Wo hast du deinen Hut, Ludwig?« Da habe ich gedacht, wie traurig sie sein möchten, wenn ich ihnen die Wahrheit sage, und ich habe gesagt, daß ich in Mühldorf eine giftige Wurst gegessen habe und daß ich froh bin, wenn ich einen Kamillentee kriege.

spoke on my behalf and asked the expediter whether people have to get arrested when they buy poisonous sausage at some train station. In the end the expediter said that I would not get arrested, but that the foot board had to get cleaned and that I had to pay for it. It cost one Mark. Then the train started again and I kept holding my head out the window to make myself feel better.

Fritz got off in Endorf, and then we arrived at my station. My mother and Annie were at the station waiting for me.

I was still feeling a little nauseous and had quite a headache.

So, I was glad that it was night time and it was not immediately obvious how pale I was. My mother gave me a kiss and asked right away: "What is this smell, Ludwig?" And Annie asked: "Where is your hat, Ludwig?" Then I thought about how sad they would be if I told them the truth, so I said that I ate some poisonous sausage in Mühldorf and that I would be glad to have some chamomile tea.

Wir sind heimgegangen, und die Lampe hat im Wohnzimmer gebrannt, und der Tisch war aufgedeckt.

Unsere alte Köchin Theres ist hergelaufen, und wie sie mich gesehen hat, da hat sie gerufen: »Jesus Maria, wie schaut unser Bub aus! Das kommt davon, weil Sie ihn so viel studieren lassen, Frau Oberförster.«

Meine Mutter sagte, daß ich etwas Unrechtes gegessen habe, und sie soll mir schnell einen Tee machen. Da ist die Theres geschwind in die Küche, und ich habe mich auf das Kanapee gesetzt. Unser Bürschel ist immer an mich hinaufgesprungen und hat mich abschlecken gewollt. Und alle haben sich gefreut, daß ich da bin. Es ist mir ganz weich geworden, und wie mich meine liebe Mutter gefragt hat, ob ich brav gewesen bin, habe ich gesagt, ja, aber ich will noch viel braver werden.

Ich sagte, wie ich die giftige Wurst drunten hatte, ist mir eingefallen, daß ich vielleicht sterben muß und daß die Leute meinen, es ist nicht schade darum. Da habe ich mir vorgenommen, daß ich jetzt anders werde und alles tue, was meiner Mutter Freude macht und viel lerne und

We went home, and the light was on in the living room, and the table was set.

Our old cook Theres came running and when she saw me she exclaimed: "Jesus and Mary, what does our boy look like! That is the result of letting him study so hard, Mrs Head Forester."

My mother said that I had eaten something bad, and she should quickly make me some tea. So Theres rushed into the kitchen and I sat down on the couch. Our Little Guy kept jumping up on me and tried to lick me. And everyone was so happy that I was there. I got all soft inside and when my dear mother asked me whether I had behaved I said yes, but I wanted to behave even better.

I said that when I had the poisonous sausage inside of me, I had had the idea that I might die and that people would not think this would be a pity. So I had resolved to become a different person and do everything to make my mother happy and I would study hard and never bring a

nie keine Strafe mehr heimbringe, daß sie alle auf mich stolz sind.

Ännchen schaute mich an und sagte: »Du hast gewiß ein furchtbar schlechtes Zeugnis heimgebracht, Ludwig?«

Aber meine Mutter hat es ihr verboten, daß sie mich ausspottet, und sie sagte: »Du sollst nicht so reden, Ännchen, wenn er doch krank war und sich vorgenommen hat, ein neues Leben zu beginnen. Er wird es schon halten und mir viele Freude machen.« Da habe ich weinen müssen, und die alte Theres hat es auch gehört, daß ich vor meinem Tod solche Vorsätze genommen habe. Sie hat furchtbar laut geweint und hat geschrien: »Es kommt von dem vielen Studieren, und sie machen unsern Buben noch kaputt.« Meine Mutter hat sie getröstet, weil sie gar nicht mehr aufgehört hat.

Da bin ich ins Bett gegangen, und es war so schön, wie ich darin gelegen bin. Meine Mutter hat noch bei der Türe hereingeleuchtet und hat gesagt: »Erhole dich recht gut, Kind.« Ich bin noch lange aufgewesen und habe gedacht, wie ich jetzt brav sein werde.

punishment home, so that everyone could be proud of me.

Annie looked at me and said: "You must have brought a terrible report card home, Ludwig?"

But my mother forbade her to tease me, and she said: "You must not talk like that, Annie, when he is not well and has resolved to begin a new life. He will keep the promise and bring me a lot of joy." That brought me to tears and the old Theres also heard that I had made such resolutions in the face of death. She wailed terribly and screamed: "This is from all this studying, and they are going to ruin our boy." My mother consoled her, because she just would not stop.

Then I went to bed and felt so good lying down. My mother shone a light through the door and said: "Now recover, my child." I lay awake for a while and thought how I would behave better from now on.

CHAPTER 6: UNCLE FRANZ

Onkel Franz

Da bekam meine Mutter einen Brief von Onkel Franz, welcher ein pensionierter Major war. Und sie sagte, daß sie recht froh ist, weil der Onkel schrieb, er will schon einen ordentlichen Menschen aus mir machen, und es kostet achtzig Mark im Monat. Dann mußte ich in die Stadt, wo Onkel wohnte. Das war sehr traurig. Es war über vier Stiegen, und es waren lauter hohe Häuser herum und kein Garten.

Uncle Franz

One day, my mother received a letter from Uncle Franz, who was a retired major. And she said she was glad, because the Uncle had written that he wanted to make a decent person out of me and it would cost eighty Marks per month. So I had to go to the city where the Uncle lives. That was very sad. It was four flights of stairs up, with high buildings all around and no yard.

17 *Bavarian officer around 1900*

Ich durfte nie spielen, und es war überhaupt niemand da. Bloß der Onkel Franz und die Tante Anna, welche den ganzen Tag herumgingen und achtgaben, daß nichts passierte. Aber der Onkel war so streng zu mir und sagte immer, wenn er mich sah: »Warte nur, du Lausbub, ich krieg dich schon noch.«

I was never allowed to play and nobody was around. Except for Uncle Franz and Aunt Anna, who walked around all day watching that nothing was happening. But the Uncle was very strict with me and every time he saw me, he said: "Just wait, you rascal, I am going to get you."

Vom Fenster aus konnte man auf die Straße hinunterspucken, und es klatschte furchtbar, wenn es danebenging. Aber wenn man die Leute traf, schauten sie zornig herum und schimpften abscheulich. Da habe ich oft gelacht, aber sonst war es gar nicht lustig.

From the window it was possible spit on the street, and there was a loud splat when you missed. But when people got hit, they looked around furiously and swore abominably. Then often had some good laughs, but otherwise there was no fun.

Der Professor konnte mich nicht leiden, weil er sagte, daß ich einen sehr schlechten Ruf mitgebracht hatte. Es war aber nicht

The Professor did not like me, because he said that I had come with a very bad reputation. But it was not true, because the report

wahr, denn das schlechte Zeugnis war bloß deswegen, weil ich der Frau Rektor ein Brausepulver in den Nachthafen getan hatte.

card had only been so bad, because I had put fizzy powder into Mrs Principal's chamber pot.

18 Nachthafen or Nachttopf = chamber pot, used for night-time urination avoiding a trip to the outhouse

Das war aber schon lang, und der Professor hätte mich nicht so schinden brauchen. Der Onkel Franz hat ihn gut gekannt und ist oft hingegangen zu ihm.

But that had occurred a long time ago, and the Professor would not have had to torment me the way he did. Uncle Franz knew him well and often went to visit him.

Dann haben sie ausgemacht, wie sie mich alle zwei erwischen können.

Then they conspired how to make my life miserable.

Wenn ich von der Schule heimkam, mußte ich mich gleich wieder hinsetzen und die Aufgaben machen.

When I came home from school, I immediately had to sit down again to do my homework.

Der Onkel schaute mir immer zu und sagte: »Machst du es wieder recht dumm? Wart nur, du Lausbub, ich komm dir schon noch.«

The Uncle kept constant watch and said: "Are you doing it real dumb again? Just wait, you rascal, I am going to get you."

Einmal mußte ich eine Arithmetikaufgabe machen. Die brachte ich nicht zusammen, und da

Once I had to do my arithmetic homework. I was unable to do it, and so I asked Uncle, because he

fragte ich den Onkel, weil er zu meiner Mutter gesagt hatte, daß er mir nachhelfen will. Und die Tante hat auch gesagt, daß der Onkel so gescheit ist und daß ich viel lernen kann bei ihm.

Deswegen habe ich ihn gebeten, daß er mir hilft, und er hat sie dann gelesen und gesagt: »Kannst du schon wieder nichts, du nichtsnutziger Lausbub? Das ist doch ganz leicht.«

Und dann hat er sich hingesetzt und hat es probiert. Es ging aber gar nicht schnell. Er rechnete den ganzen Nachmittag, und wie ich ihn fragte, ob er es noch nicht fertig hat, schimpfte er mich fürchterlich und war sehr grob. Erst vor dem Essen brachte er mir die Rechnung und sagte: »Jetzt kannst du es abschreiben; es war doch ganz leicht, aber ich habe noch etwas anderes tun müssen, du Dummkopf.«

Ich habe es abgeschrieben und dem Professor gegeben. Am Donnerstag kam die Aufgabe heraus, und ich meinte, daß ich einen Einser kriege. Es war aber wieder ein Vierer, und das ganze Blatt war rot, und der Professor sagte: »So eine dumme Rechnung kann bloß ein Esel machen.«

had told my mother that he would tutor me. The Aunt had also said that the Uncle was so smart and that I would be able to learn a lot from him.

This is why I asked him to help me and he read the question and said: "You can't do it again, you good-for-nothing rascal? But that's so easy."

And then he sat down and tried. But it did not go quickly. He calculated the whole afternoon and when I asked him whether he was done, he scolded me terribly and was being very rough. Just before dinner, he brought the calculation to me and said: "Now you can copy it; it was really easy, but I had other things to do too, you dummy."

I copied it and gave it to the Professor. On Thursday, he returned the homework and I thought I would get an A. But it was a D again and the whole piece of paper was all marked up in red and the Professor said: "Such a dumb calculation can only be done by an ass."

»Das war mein Onkel«, sagte ich, »der hat es gemacht, und ich habe es bloß abgeschrieben.«

Die ganze Klasse hat gelacht, und der Professor wurde aber rot.

»Du bist ein gemeiner Lügner«, sagte er, »und du wirst noch im Zuchthaus enden.« Dann sperrte er mich zwei Stunden ein. Der Onkel wartete schon auf mich, weil er mich durchhaute, wenn ich eingesperrt war. Ich schrie aber gleich, daß er schuld ist, weil er die Rechnung so falsch gemacht hat, und daß der Professor gesagt hat, so was kann bloß ein Esel machen.

Da haute er mich erst recht durch, und dann ging er fort. Der Greither Heinrich, mein Freund, hat ihn gesehen, wie er auf der Straße mit dem Professor gegangen ist und wie sie immer stehenblieben und der Onkel recht eifrig geredet hat.

Am nächsten Tag hat mich der Professor aufgerufen und sagte: »Ich habe deine Rechnung noch einmal durchgelesen; sie ist ganz richtig, aber nach einer alten Methode, welche es nicht mehr gibt. Es schadet dir aber nichts, daß du eingesperrt warst, weil du es eigentlich immer verdienst, und weil du beim Abschreiben Fehler gemacht hast.«

"That was my uncle," I said, "he did it and I only copied it."

The whole class was laughing, and the Professor got all red in the face.

"You are a mean liar," he said, "and you will end up in jail." Then he locked me up for two hours. The Uncle was already waiting for me, because he always gave me a beating me when I had been locked up. But I immediately started screaming that it was his fault because he had calculated it all wrong and the Professor had said that only an ass could do it like that.

Then he gave me an extra hard beating and left. Greither's Heinrich, my friend, had seen him walk on the street with the Professor and they often stopped and the Uncle had been talking very agitatedly.

The next day, the Professor called me up and said: "I have looked through your calculation again; it is all correct, but it was done with an old method that is not in use anymore. It does not hurt you to have been locked up though, because you always tend to deserve it, and because you made mistakes in copying."

Das haben sie miteinander ausgemacht, denn der Onkel sagte gleich, wie ich heimkam: »Ich habe mit deinem Professor gesprochen. Die Rechnung war schon gut, aber du hast beim Abschreiben nicht aufgepaßt, du Lausbub.«

Ich habe schon aufgepaßt, es war nur ganz falsch.

Aber meine Mutter schrieb mir, daß ihr der Onkel geschrieben hat, daß er mir nicht mehr nachhelfen kann, weil ich die einfachsten Rechnungen nicht abschreiben kann und weil er dadurch in Verlegenheit kommt. Das ist ein gemeiner Mensch.

They had agreed on doing this, because the Uncle told me as soon as I came home: "I had a word with your Professor. The calculation was correct, but you did not pay attention when you copied it, you rascal."

However, I had paid attention, it had just been completely wrong.

But my mother wrote me that the Uncle had written her that he could not tutor me anymore, because I was unable to copy the simplest calculations and thus caused him embarrassment. That is a mean person.

CHAPTER 7: PERJURY

Der Meineid

Werners Heinrich sagte, seine Mama hat ihm den Umgang mit mir verboten, weil ich so was Rohes in meinem Benehmen habe und weil ich doch bald davongejagt werde. Ich sagte zu Werners Heinrich, daß ich auf seine Mama pfeife, und ich bin froh, wenn ich nicht hin muß, weil es in seinem Zimmer so muffelt.

Dann sagte er, ich bin ein gemeiner Kerl, und ich gab ihm eine feste auf die Backe und ich schmiß ihn an den Ofenschirm, daß er hinfiel.

Perjury

Werner's Heinrich said his Mama had forbidden him to be with me, because I had such rough manners and would get chased off soon anyway. I told Werner's Heinrich that I did not give a rip for his Mama and that I was glad not to come visit him, because it reeks in his room.

Then he said that I was a mean guy and I slapped him across the face and pushed him against the fireplace screen that he fell down.

19 *metal fireplace screen: prevents sparks from flying into the room and helps distribute the heat*

Und dann war ihm ein Zahn gebrochen, und die Samthose hatte ein großes Loch über dem Knie.

Am Nachmittag kam der Pedell in unsere Klasse und meldete, daß ich zum Herrn Rektor hinunter soll.

Ich ging hinaus und schnitt bei der Tür eine Grimasse, daß alle lachen mußten. Es hat mich aber keiner verschuftet, weil sie schon wußten, daß ich es ihnen heimzahlen würde. Werners Heinrich hat es nicht gesehen, weil er daheim blieb, weil er den Zahn nicht mehr hatte.

Sonst hätte er mich schon verschuftet.

And then one of his teeth was broken and the velvet pants had a large hole above the knee.

That afternoon, the janitor came into our classroom and declared that I had to go down to see Mr Principal.

I walked out and made a face by the door that made everyone burst out laughing. But nobody ratted me out because they already knew that I would have paid it back to them. Werner's Heinrich did not see it, because he had stayed home, due to the fact that his tooth was missing.

Otherwise he would have ratted me out.

Ich mußte gleich zum Herrn Rektor hinein, der mich mit seinen grünen Augen sehr scharf ansah.

I had to immediately go into Mr Principal's office, who closely examined me with his green eyes.

»Da bist du schon wieder, ungezogener Bube«, sagte er, »wirst du uns nie von deiner Gegenwart befreien?«

"There you are again, you naughty boy," he said, "will you never rid us of your presence?"

Ich dachte mir, daß ich sehr froh sein möchte, wenn ich den ekelhaften Kerl nicht mehr sehen muß, aber er hatte mich doch selber gerufen.

I thought to myself that I would be delighted not to see this disgusting guy ever again, but he had called me himself after all.

»Was willst du eigentlich werden«, fragte er, »du verrohtes Subjekt? Glaubst du, daß du jemals die humanistischen Studien vollenden kannst?«

"What do you want do with your life," he asked, "you degenerate subject? Do you believe that you will ever be able to complete your humanistic studies?"

Ich sagte, daß ich das schon glaube. Da fuhr er mich aber an und schrie so laut, daß es der Pedell draußen hörte und es allen erzählte. Er sagte, daß ich eine Verbrechernatur habe und eine katilinarische Existenz bin und daß ich höchstens ein gemeiner Handwerker werde und daß schon im Altertum alle verworfenen Menschen so angefangen haben wie ich.

I said that did believe that I would be able to. Then he tore into me and screamed so loud that the janitor could hear it outside and told everyone about it. He said that I was of criminal nature and a Catilinian existence and that I would at most become a common handyman and that depraved people had started out like this even in antiquity.

»Der Herr Ministerialrat Werner war bei mir«, sagte er, »und schilderte mir den bemitleidenswerten Zustand seines Sohnes«, und dann gab er mir sechs Stunden Karzer als Rektoratsstrafe wegen

"Mr Undersecretary Werner came to see me," he said, "and informed me about his son's pitiful condition," and then he gave me six hours of detention as the

entsetzlicher Roheit. Und meine Mutter bekam eine Rechnung vom Herrn Ministerialrat, daß sie achtzehn Mark bezahlen mußte für die Hose.

Sie weinte sehr stark, nicht wegen dem Geld, obwohl sie fast keines hatte, sondern weil ich immer wieder was anfange. Ich ärgerte mich furchtbar, daß meine Mutter soviel Kummer hatte, und nahm mir vor, daß es Werners Heinrich nicht gut gehen soll.

Die zerrissene Hose hat uns der Herr Ministerialrat nicht gegeben, obwohl er eine neue verlangte.

Am nächsten Sonntag nach der Kirche wurde ich auf dem Rektorat eingesperrt. Das war fad.

In dem Zimmer waren die zwei Söhne vom Herrn Rektor. Der eine mußte übersetzen und hatte lauter dicke Bücher auf seinem Tische, in denen er nachschlagen mußte. Jedesmal, wenn sein Vater hereinkam, blätterte er furchtbar schnell um und fuhr mit dem Kopfe auf und ab.

»Was suchst du, mein Sohn?« fragte der Rektor. Er antwortete nicht gleich, weil er ein Trumm Brot im Munde hatte. Er schluckte es aber doch hinunter

Principal's punishment for terrible roughness. And my mother received from Mr Undersecretary a bill over eighteen Marks for the pants.

She cried a lot, not because of the money of which she had almost none, but because I always got into trouble. I got terribly angry that my mother had so much grief, and I resolved to ensure that Werner's Heinrich should not fare well.

Mr Undersecretary did not give us the torn pants, even though he had demanded a new one.

The following Sunday, after church, I got locked into the principal's office. That was boring.

The Principal's two sons were in the room. One of them was working on a translation and had lots of thick books on the table for looking things up. Every time his father came in, he furiously turned pages and moved his head up and down.

"What are you looking for, my son?" asked the Principal. He did not answer right away, because he had a huge chunk of bread in his mouth. He finally swallowed

und sagte, daß er ein griechisches Wort sucht, welches er nicht finden kann. Es war aber nicht wahr; er hatte gar nicht gesucht, weil er immer Brot aus der Tasche aß. Ich habe es ganz gut gesehen.

Der Rektor lobte ihn aber doch und sagte, daß die Götter den Schweiß vor die Tugend hinstellen, oder so was.

Dann ging er zum andern Sohn, welcher an einer Staffelei stand und zeichnete. Das Bild war schon beinah fertig. Es war eine Landschaft mit einem See und viele Schiffe darauf. Die Frau Rektor kam auch herein und sah es an, und der Rektor war sehr lustig. Er sagte, daß es bei dem Schlußfeste ausgestellt wird, und daß alle Besucher sehen können, daß die schönen Künste gepflegt werden.

Dann gingen sie, und die zwei Söhne gingen auch, weil es zum Essen Zeit war. Ich mußte allein bleiben und bekam nichts zu essen.

Ich machte mir aber nichts daraus, weil ich eine Salami bei mir hatte, und ich dachte mir, daß die zwei dürren Rektorssöhne froh wären, wenn sie so viel kriegten.

Der Ältere stellte sein Bild an das Fenster im Nebenzimmer. Das

it and said that he was looking for a Greek word but was unable to find it. However, this was not true; he had not been looking for anything, because he kept eating bread from his pocket. I saw it very well.

The Principal commended him anyway and said that the Gods prefer sweat over virtue, or something like that.

Then he went to the other son, who stood in front of an easel and was drawing. The picture was almost done. It showed a landscape with a lake and many ships. Mrs Principal also came in and looked at it, and the Principal was very cheerful. He said that it would be exhibited at the final celebration and that all visitors would be able to see what beautiful arts were being practiced.

Then they left, and the two sons left as well, because it was time for lunch. I had to stay by myself and did not get anything to eat.

But I did not care, because I had a salami along, and I thought that the two scrawny principal sons would be glad to get so much.

The older one put his picture next to the window in the other

sah ich genau. Ich wartete, bis alle draußen waren, und las dann die Geschichte vom schwarzen Apachenwolf weiter, die ich heimlich dabei hatte.

Um vier Uhr wurde ich herausgelassen vom Pedell. Er sagte: »So, diesmal warst du aber feste drin.« Ich sagte: »Das macht mir gar nichts.« Es machte mir aber schon etwas, weil es so furchtbar fad war. Am Montagnachmittag kam der Rektor in die Klasse und hatte einen ganz roten Kopf.

Er schrie, gleich wie er herein war: »Wo ist der Thoma?« Ich stand auf. Dann ging es an. Er sagte, ich habe ein Verbrechen begangen, welches in den Annalen der Schule unerhört ist, eine herostratische Tat, die gleich nach dem Brande des Dianatempels kommt. Und ich kann meine Lage nur durch ein reumütiges Geständnis einigermaßen verbessern.

Dabei riß er den Mund auf, daß man seine abscheulichen Zähne sah, und spuckte furchtbar und rollte seine Augen.

Ich sagte: »Ich weiß nichts; ich habe doch gar nichts getan.«

Er hieß mich einen verruchten Lügner, der den Zorn des Himmels auf sich zieht. Aber ich sagte: »Ich weiß doch gar nichts.«

room. I saw it clearly. I waited until everyone was gone, and then I kept reading the story of the black Apache wolf that I had secretly brought in.

At four o'clock, I was let go by the janitor. He said: "So, this time you were down tight." I said: "I'm not bothered at all." But I was bothered, because it had been terribly boring. On Monday afternoon, the Principal came into the class room and had a very red head.

As soon as he was in, he screamed: "Where is Thoma?" I stood up. Then it began. He said that I had committed a crime that was unheard of in the annals of the school, a herostratic deed that nearly rivaled burning down the temple of Diana. And I would only be able to somewhat improve my situation by confessing ruefully.

With this, he opened his mouth so wide that one could see his abhorrent teeth, and he spit terribly and rolled his eyes.

I said: "I don't know anything; I didn't do anything."

He called me a wicked liar who pulls the wrath of the Heavens onto himself. But I said: "But I don't know anything."

Und dann fragte er alle in der Klasse, ob sie nichts gegen mich aussagen können, aber niemand wußte nichts.

Und dann sagte er es unserem Professor. In der Frühe sah man, daß im Zimmer neben dem Rektorat das Fenster eingeschmissen war, und ein großer Stein lag am Boden, der war auch durch das Bild gegangen, welches der Sohn gemalt hatte, und es war kaputt und lag auf dem Boden.

Unser Professor war ganz entsetzt, und sein Bart und seine Haare standen in die Höhe. Er fuhr auf mich los und brüllte: »Gestehe es, Verruchter, hast du diese schändliche Tat begangen?« Ich sagte, ich weiß doch gar nichts, das wird mir schon zu arg, daß ich alles getan haben muß.

Der Rektor schrie wieder: »Wehe dir, dreimal wehe! Wenn ich dich entdecke! Es kommt doch an die Sonne.«

Und dann ging er hinaus. Und nach einer Stunde kam der Pedell und holte mich auf das Rektorat. Da war schon unser Religionslehrer da und der Rektor. Das Bild lag auf einem Stuhl und der Stein auch. Davor stand ein kleiner Tisch. Der war mit einem schwarzen Tuch bedeckt, und

And then he asked everyone in the class whether they could make a statement against me, but nobody knew of anything.

And then he told our Professor. Early in the morning they had found that the window in the room next to the Principal's office had been thrown in, and a large rock lay on the floor which had also passed through the picture drawn by the son, and it was broken and lay on the floor.

Our Professor was all horrified, and his beard and hair stood up straight. He tore into me and yelled: "Admit it, wicked one, have you committed this heinous act?" I said I did not know of anything; it was going too far how I was supposed to have done everything.

The Principal screamed again: "Woe unto you, thrice woe! When I discover your guilt! It will come out into the open."

And then he left. And one hour later, the janitor came and took me to the Principal's office. Our religion teacher was already there and the Principal. The picture lay on a chair and the rock as well. In front of that stood a little table. It was covered with a black cloth, and there were two burning candles and a crucifix.

zwei brennende Kerzen waren
da und ein Kruzifix.

20 *Simplicissimus 1905, #32, p. 376*

Der Religionslehrer legte seine Hand auf meinen Kopf und tat recht gütig, obwohl er mich sonst gar nicht leiden konnte.

»Du armer, verblendeter Junge«, sagte er, »nun schütte dein Herz aus und gestehe mir alles. Es wird dir wohltun und dein Gewissen erleichtern.«

»Und es wird deine Lage verbessern«, sagte der Rektor.

»Ich war es doch gar nicht. Ich habe doch gar kein Fenster nicht hineingeschmissen«, sagte ich.

Der Religionslehrer sah jetzt sehr böse aus. Dann sagte er zum Rektor: »Wir werden jetzt sofort Klarheit haben. Das Mittel hilft bestimmt.« Er führte mich zum

The Religion teacher laid his hand on my head and acted all benevolent, even though he could not stand me otherwise.

"You poor, deluded boy," he said, "now pour out your heart and confess everything to me. It will do you well and relieve your conscience."

"And it will improve your situation," said the Principal.

"But I didn't do it. I did not throw in no window," I said.

The Religion teacher now looked furious. Then he said to the Principal: "We will clear this up immediately. This measure will surely help." He led me to

Tische, vor die Kerzen hin, und sagte furchtbar feierlich:

»Nun frage ich dich vor diesen brennenden Lichtern. Du kennst die schrecklichen Folgen des Meineides vom Religionsunterrichte. Ich frage dich: Hast du den Stein hineingeworfen? Ja — oder nein?«

»Ich habe doch gar keinen Stein nicht hineingeschmissen«, sagte ich.

»Antworte ja — oder nein, im Namen alles Heiligen!«

»Nein«, sagte ich.

Der Religionslehrer zuckte die Achseln und sagte: »Nun war er es doch nicht. Der Schein trügt.«

Dann schickte mich der Rektor fort.

Ich bin recht froh, daß ich gelogen habe und nichts eingestand, daß ich am Sonntagabend den Stein hineinschmiß, wo ich wußte, daß das Bild war. Denn ich hätte meine Lage gar nicht verbessert und wäre davongejagt worden. Das sagte der Rektor bloß so. Aber ich bin nicht so dumm.

the table, in front of the candles, and said terribly solemnly:

"Now I ask you in front of these burning lights. You know the terrible consequences of perjury from religion instruction. I ask you: Did you throw the rock? Yes - or no?"

"But I did not throw no rock," I said.

"Answer yes - or no, in the name of everything Holy!"

"No," I said.

The Religion teacher shrugged his shoulders and said: "Now it wasn't him after all. Appearances are deceptive."

The Principal sent me away.

I am quite glad that I lied and did not confess having thrown the rock on Sunday evening where I knew that the picture was. Because I would not have improved my situation and would have been chased off. The Principal just said those things. But I am not that stupid.

CHAPTER 8: THE ENGAGEMENT

Die Verlobung

The Engagement

Unser Klaßprofessor Bindinger hatte es auf meine Schwester Marie abgesehen.

Our class teacher Bindinger had an eye on my sister Marie.

Ich merkte es bald, aber daheim taten alle so geheimnisvoll, daß ich nichts erfahre.

I noticed this right away, but at home everybody was all secretive, so that I would not find out.

Sonst hat Marie immer mit mir geschimpft, und wenn meine Mutter sagte: »Ach Gott, ja!«, mußte sie immer noch was dazutun und sagte, ich bin ein nichtsnutziger Lausbub. Auf einmal wurde sie ganz sanft. Wenn ich in die Klasse ging, lief sie mir oft bis an die Treppe nach und sagte: »Magst du keinen Apfel mitnehmen, Ludwig?« Und dann gab sie Obacht, daß ich einen weißen Kragen anhatte, und band mir die Krawatte, wenn ich es nicht recht gemacht hatte.

At other times, Marie had always scolded me and when my mother said: "Oh God, now!" she always had to add something to that calling me a good-for-nothing rascal. Suddenly she turned all meek. When I went into the class room, she often followed me all the way to the stairs and said: "Don't you want to take an apple, Ludwig?" And then she made sure that I was wearing a white collar, and she tied my tie if I had not done it quite right.

Einmal kaufte sie mir eine neue, und sonst hat sie sich nie darum gekümmert. Das kam mir gleich

Once she bought me a new one, although she had otherwise never paid attention to that. I im-

verdächtig vor, aber ich wußte nicht, warum sie es tat.

mediately thought this was suspicious, but I did not know why she was doing this.

Wenn ich heimkam, fragte sie mich oft: »Hat dich der Herr Professor aufgerufen? Ist der Herr Professor freundlich zu dir?«

When I came home, she often asked me: "Did Mr Professor call on you? Is Mr Professor nice to you?"

»Was geht denn dich das an?« sagte ich. »Tu nicht gar so gescheit! Auf dich pfeife ich!«

"What is it to you?" I said. "Don't act so clever! I don't care about you!"

Ich meinte zuerst, das ist eine neue Mode von ihr, weil die Mädel alle Augenblicke was anderes haben, daß sie recht gescheit aussehen. Hinterher habe ich mich erst ausgekannt.

At first I thought this was a new fad of hers, because the girls constantly come up with something new to make themselves look clever. I figured it out only much later.

Der Bindinger konnte mich nie leiden, und ich ihn auch nicht. Er war so dreckig.

Bindinger could never stand me and I not him either. He was so dirty.

Zum Frühstück hat er immer weiche Eier gegessen; das sah man, weil sein Bart voll Dotter war.

For breakfast, he always had soft-boiled eggs; this was visible, because his beard was full of yolk.

Er spuckte einen an, wenn er redete, und seine Augen waren so grün wie von einer Katze. Alle Professoren sind dumm, aber er war noch dümmer.

He spit at you when he talked, and his eyes were as green as that of a cat. All Professors were dumb, but he was even dumber.

Die Haare ließ er sich auch nicht schneiden und hatte viele Schuppen.

He never had his hair cut, and he had lots of dandruff.

Wenn er von den alten Deutschen redete, strich er seinen

Whenever he talked of the old Germans, he stroked his beard and talked with a bass voice.

Bart und machte sich eine Baß-
stimme.

Ich glaube aber nicht, daß sie einen solchen Bauch hatten und so
abgelatschte Stiefel wie er.

But I do not believe that they
had a big belly like him and such
worn-out boots.

Die andern schimpfte er, aber
mich sperrte er ein, und er sagte
immer: »Du wirst nie ein nützliches Glied der Gesellschaft,
elender Bursche!«

He scolded the others, but me he
locked up, and he always said:
"You will never be a productive
member of society, miserable
scoundrel!"

Dann war ein Ball in der Liedertafel, wo meine Mutter auch hin-
ging wegen der Marie.

Then there was a dance at the
Liedertafel tavern, which my
mother also attended because of
Marie.

Sie kriegte ein Rosakleid dazu
und heulte furchtbar, weil die
Näherin so spät fertig wurde.

She got a pink dress for this and
cried terribly, because the seamstress did not finish until very
late.

Ich war froh, wie sie draußen waren mit dem Getue.

I was glad when they took their
drama outside.

Am andern Tage beim Essen redete sie vom Balle und Marie
sagte zu mir: »Du, Ludwig, Herr
Professor Bindinger war auch
da. Nein, das ist ein reizender
Mensch!«

The next day, they talked about
the dance during dinner and Marie told me: "Listen, Ludwig, Mr
Professor Bindinger was there as
well. Well, that is a charming person!"

Das ärgerte mich, und ich fragte
sie, ob er recht gespuckt hat und
ob er ihr Rosakleid nicht voll Ei-
erflecken gemacht hat. Sie wurde
ganz rot, und auf einmal sprang
sie in die Höhe und lief hinaus,
und man hörte durch die Tür,
wie sie weinte.

That ticked me off, and I asked
her whether he had spit real
nicely and gotten egg stains on
her pink dress. She blushed and
suddenly she jumped up and ran
out, and her crying was audible
through the door.

21 Simplicissimus, 1896, #34, p. 8

Ich mußte glauben, daß sie verrückt ist, aber meine Mutter sagte sehr böse: »Du sollst nicht unanständig reden von deinen Lehrern; das kann Mariechen nicht ertragen.«

»Ich möchte schon wissen, was es sie angeht, das ist doch dumm, daß sie deswegen weint.« »Mariechen ist ein gutes Kind«, sagte meine Mutter, »und sie sieht, was ich leiden muß, wenn du nichts lernst und unanständig bist gegen deinen Professor.«

»Er hat aber doch den ganzen Bart voll lauter Eidotter«, sagte ich.

I had to believe that she had gone mad, but my mother said very angrily: "You must not speak disrespectfully of your teachers; dear Marie cannot handle that."

"I would like to know why that is any of her business; it is stupid that she cries because of that." "Dear Marie is a good child," my mother said, "and she sees how it griefs me when you do not learn and misbehave towards your Professor."

"But his beard is full of egg yolk," I said.

»Er ist ein sehr braver und gescheiter Mann, der noch eine große Laufbahn hat. Und er war sehr nett zu Mariechen. Und er hat ihr auch gesagt, wieviel Sorgen du ihm machst. Und jetzt bist du ruhig!«

"He is a decent and intelligent man who will have a great career. And he was very nice to little Marie. And he also told her how much worry you are causing him. And now be quiet!"

Ich sagte nichts mehr, aber ich dachte, was der Bindinger für ein Kerl ist, daß er mich bei meiner Schwester verschuftet.

I did not say anything anymore, but I thought what kind of guy Bindinger was that he talked bad about me to my sister.

Am Nachmittag hat er mich aufgerufen; ich habe aber den Nepos nicht präpariert gehabt und konnte nicht übersetzen.

This afternoon, he called on me; but I had not prepared the Nepos text and was unable to translate.

C. NEPOS, Veronenſis.

»Warum bist du schon wieder unvorbereitet, Bursche?« fragte er.

"Why are you unprepared again, man?" he asked.

Ich wußte zuerst keine Ausrede und sagte: »Entschuldigen, Herr Professor, ich habe nicht gekonnt.«

»Was hast du nicht gekonnt?«

»Ich habe keinen Nepos nicht präparieren gekonnt, weil meine Schwester auf dem Ball war.«

»Das ist doch der Gipfel der Unverfrorenheit, mit einer so törichten Entschuldigung zu kommen«, sagte er, aber ich habe mich schon auf etwas besonnen und sagte, daß ich so Kopfweh gehabt habe, weil die Näherin so lange nicht gekommen war und weil ich sie holen mußte und auf der Stiege ausrutschte und mit dem Kopf aufschlug und furchtbare Schmerzen hatte.

Ich dachte mir, wenn er es nicht glaubt, ist es mir auch wurscht, weil er es nicht beweisen kann.

Er schimpfte mich aber nicht und ließ mich gehen.

Einen Tag danach, wie ich aus der Klasse kam, saß die Marie auf dem Kanapee im Wohnzimmer und heulte furchtbar. Und meine Mutter hielt ihr den Kopf und sagte: »Das wird schon, Mariechen. Sei ruhig, Kindchen!«

»Nein, es wird niemals, ganz gewiß nicht, der Lausbub tut es mit

At first I could not think of an excuse and said: "Excuse me, Mr Professor, but I couldn't."

"You couldn't do what?"

"I couldn't prepare no Nepos, because my sister went to the dance."

"That is the height of insolence, to come with such a foolish excuse," he said, but I had already thought of something and said that I had had such a headache, because the seamstress had been very late such that I had to go get her and slipped on the stairs and hit my head and got terrible pains.

I thought that if he did not believe it, I would not care, because he could not prove anything.

However, he did not scold me and let me go.

The next day, I came home from school and Marie was sitting on the sofa in the living room and was crying horribly. And my mother was holding her head and said: "It'll all work out, little Marie. Calm down, my child."

"No, it won't ever, for sure not, the rascal is trying hard to make me miserable."

Fleiß, daß ich unglücklich werde.«

»Was hat sie denn schon wieder für eine Heulerei?« fragte ich.

Da wurde meine Mutter so zornig, wie ich sie gar nie gesehen habe.

»Du sollst noch fragen!« sagte sie. »Du kannst es nicht vor Gott verantworten, was du deiner Schwester tust, und nicht genug, daß du faul bist, redest du dich auf das arme Mädchen aus und sagst, du wärst über die Stiege gefallen, weil du für sie zur Näherin mußtest. Was soll der gute Professor Bindinger von uns denken?«

»Er wird meinen, daß wir ihn bloß ausnützen! Er wird meinen, daß wir alle lügen, er wird glauben, ich bin auch so!« schrie Marie und drückte wieder ihr nasses Tuch auf die Augen.

Ich ging gleich hinaus, weil ich schon wußte, daß sie noch ärger tut, wenn ich dabeiblieb, und ich kriegte das Essen auf mein Zimmer.

Das war an einem Freitag; und am Sonntag kam auf einmal meine Mutter zu mir herein und lachte so freundlich und sagte, ich soll in das Wohnzimmer kommen.

"What is all this wailing again?" I asked.

This made my mother furious like I had never seen her before.

"You should ask!" she said. "You cannot justify before God what you are doing to your sister, and it's not enough that you are lazy, but you use the poor girl as an excuse and say you had fallen on the stairs because you had to go to the seamstress for her. What should good Professor Bindinger think of us?"

"He will think that we just take advantage of him! He will think that we all lie; he will think I am like this too!" Marie exclaimed and held her wet handkerchief against her eyes again.

I left the room, because I knew that she would lose it even more if I stayed, and I got my dinner in my room.

That was on a Friday; and on Sunday my mother suddenly came into my room and smiled happily and said I should come into the living room.

Da stand der Herr Professor Bindinger, und Marie hatte den Kopf bei ihm angelehnt, und er schielte furchtbar. Meine Mutter führte mich bei der Hand und sagte: »Ludwig, unsere Marie wird jetzt deine Frau Professor«, und dann nahm sie ihr Taschentuch heraus und weinte. Und Marie weinte. Der Bindinger ging zu mir und legte seine Hand auf meinen Kopf und sagte: »Wir wollen ein nützliches Glied der Gesellschaft aus ihm machen.«

There stood Mr Professor Bindinger and Marie was leaning her head against him and he looked terribly cross-eyed. My mother took me by the hand and said: "Ludwig, our Marie will now become your Mr Professor," and then she pulled out her handkerchief and cried. And Marie cried. Bindinger approached me and laid his hand on my head and said: "Let us make him a productive member of society."

CHAPTER 9: GRETCHEN VOLLBECK

Gretchen Vollbeck

Von meinem Zimmer aus konnte ich in den Vollbeckschen Garten sehen, weil die Rückseite unseres Hauses gegen die Korngasse hinausging.

Wenn ich nachmittags meine Schulaufgaben machte, sah ich Herrn Rat Vollbeck mit seiner Frau beim Kaffee sitzen, und ich hörte fast jedes Wort, das sie sprachen.

Er fragte immer: »Wo ist denn nur unser Gretchen so lange?«, und sie antwortete alle Tage: »Ach Gott, das arme Kind studiert wieder einmal.«

Ich hatte damals, wie heute, kein Verständnis dafür, daß ein Mensch gerne studiert und sich dadurch vom Kaffeetrinken oder irgend etwas anderem abhalten lassen kann. Dennoch machte es einen großen Eindruck auf mich, obwohl ich dies nie eingestand.

Gretchen Vollbeck

From my room I was able to look into the Vollbecks' backyard, because the back of our house faced the Korngasse.

When I did my homework in the afternoons, I could always see Mr Councilor Vollbeck having coffee with his wife, and I was able to hear almost every word they spoke.

He always asked: "Where could our Gretchen be for such a long time?," and every day she responded: "Oh Lord, the poor child is studying again."

Back then, just like today, I had no idea why somebody would enjoy studying and allow it to interfere with having coffee or doing anything else. Nevertheless, I was deeply impressed, although I never admitted that.

Wir sprachen im Gymnasium öfters von Gretchen Vollbeck, und ich verteidigte sie nie, wenn einer erklärte, sie sei eine ekelhafte Gans, die sich bloß gescheit mache.

At the Gymnasium, we often talked about Gretchen Vollbeck, and I never sprung to her defense when somebody declared she was a disgusting goose that just wanted to appear smart.

Auch daheim äußerte ich mich einmal wegwerfend über dieses weibliche Wesen, das wahrscheinlich keinen Strumpf stricken könne und sich den Kopf mit allem möglichen Zeug vollpfropfe.

At home, I also once made a deprecating remark about this female being who was probably unable to mend a sock and filled her head with all kinds of stuff.

Meine Mutter unterbrach mich aber mit der Bemerkung, sie würde Gott danken, wenn ein gewisser Jemand nur halb so fleißig wäre wie dieses talentierte Mädchen, das seinen Eltern nur Freude bereite und sicherlich nie so schmachvolle Schulzeugnisse heimbringe.

My mother interrupted me with the remark that she would thank God if a certain someone would only be half as diligent as this talented girl who is just a joy to her parents and certainly never brings such pitiful report cards home.

Ich haßte persönliche Anspielungen und vermied es daher, das Gespräch auf dieses unangenehme Thema zu bringen.

I hated such personal allusions and thus avoided mentioning this unpleasant subject.

Dagegen übte meine Mutter nicht die gleiche Rücksicht, und ich wurde häufig aufgefordert, mir an Gretchen Vollbeck ein Beispiel zu nehmen.

My mother, however, was not that considerate, and I was often told to take Gretchen Vollbeck as an example.

Ich tat es nicht und brachte an Ostern ein Zeugnis heim, welches selbst den nächsten Verwandten nicht gezeigt werden konnte. Man drohte mir, daß ich

I did not do that and for Easter, I brought a report card home that could not even be shown to the closest relatives. I was threatened with having to take up an

nächster Tage zu einem Schuster in die Lehre gegeben würde, und als ich gegen dieses ehrbare Handwerk keine Abneigung zeigte, erwuchsen mir sogar daraus heftige Vorwürfe.

Es folgten recht unerquickliche Tage, und jedermann im Hause war bemüht, mich so zu behandeln, daß in mir keine rechte Festesfreude aufkommen konnte.

Schließlich sagte meine Mutter, sie sehe nur noch ein Mittel, mich auf bessere Wege zu bringen, und dies sei der Umgang mit Gretchen.

Vielleicht gelinge es dem Mädchen, günstig auf mich einzuwirken. Herr Rat Vollbeck habe seine Zustimmung erteilt, und ich solle mich bereit halten, den Nachmittag mit ihr hinüberzugehen.

Die Sache war mir unangenehm. Man verkehrt als Lateinschüler nicht so gerne mit Mädchen wie später, und außerdem hatte ich begründete Furcht, daß gewisse Gegensätze zu stark hervorgehoben würden.

Aber da half nun einmal nichts, ich mußte mit.

Vollbecks saßen gerade beim Kaffee, als wir kamen. Gretchen

apprenticeship with a shoemaker soon, and when I did not exhibit any aversion against this venerable craft, this earned me more severe rebuke.

The following days were rather unenjoyable, and everybody in the house went out of their way to treat me such that I did not get into a real festive mood.

Finally, my mother said she did not see any other means for bringing me on better paths than being in the company of Gretchen.

Maybe the girl would be able to exert positive influence on me. Mr Councilor Vollbeck had agreed and I was to keep myself ready to spend the afternoon at her place.

This situation made me uncomfortable. As a Latin student, one does not converse with girls as much as one would later in life, and I was moreover reasonably worried that certain contrasts would be emphasized excessively.

But as there was nothing to be done, I had to go along.

The Vollbecks were just having coffee when we arrived.

fehlte, und Frau Rat sagte gleich: »Ach Gott, das Mädchen studiert schon wieder, und noch dazu Scheologie.« Meine Mutter nickte so nachdenklich und ernst mit dem Kopfe, daß mir wirklich ein Stich durchs Herz ging und der Gedanke in mir auftauchte, der lieben alten Frau doch auch einmal eine Freude zu machen. Der Herr Rat trommelte mit den Fingern auf den Tisch und zog die Augenbrauen furchtbar in die Höhe.

Dann sagte er: »Ja, ja, die Scheologie!«

Jetzt glaubte meine Mutter, daß es Zeit sei, mich ein bißchen in das Licht zu rücken, und sie fragte mich aufmunternd: »Habt ihr das auch in eurer Klasse?«

Frau Rat Vollbeck lächelte über die Zumutung, daß anderer Leute Kinder derartiges lernten, und ihr Mann sah mich durchbohrend an; das ärgerte mich so stark, daß ich beschloß, ihnen eins zu geben.

»Es heißt gar nicht Scheologie, sondern Geologie, und das braucht man nicht zu lernen«, sagte ich.

Beinahe hätte mich diese Bemerkung gereut, als ich die große Verlegenheit meiner Mutter sah;

Gretchen was missing, and Mrs Councilor immediately said: "Dear Lord, the girl is studying again, and Chiology on top of that." My mother nodded her head so pensively and seriously that it made me sick at heart and the thought appeared within me to for once bring some joy to the dear old woman. Mr Councilor was drumming on the table with his fingers and raised his eyebrows to terrible heights.

Then he said: "Yes, yes, Chiology!"

Now my mother thought it was time to bring me into the light and asked me encouragingly: "Do you have that in your class too?"

Mrs Councilor Vollbeck smiled upon the impertinence that other people's children should learn anything of the like, and her husband looked at me with piercing eyes; that angered me so much that I decided to give them an earful.

"It is not called Chiology, but Geology, and nobody needs to learn stuff like that," I said.

I almost regretted this remark when I saw my mother's deep embarrassment; she was clearly

sie mochte sich wohl sehr über mich schämen, und sie hatte Tränen in den Augen, als Herr Vollbeck sie mit einem recht schmerzlichen Mitleid ansah.

Der alte Esel schnitt eine Menge Grimassen, von denen jede bedeuten sollte, daß er sehr trübe in meine Zukunft sehe.

»Du scheinst der Ansicht zu sein«, sagte er zu mir, »daß man sehr vieles nicht lernen muß. Dein Osterzeugnis soll ja nicht ganz zur Zufriedenheit deiner beklagenswerten Frau Mutter ausgefallen sein. Übrigens konnte man zu meiner Zeit auch Scheologie sagen.«

Ich war durch diese Worte nicht so vernichtet, wie Herr Vollbeck annahm, aber ich war doch froh, daß Gretchen ankam. Sie wurde von ihren Eltern stürmisch begrüßt, ganz anders wie sonst, wenn ich von meinem Fenster aus zusah. Sie wollten meiner Mutter zeigen, eine wie große Freude die Eltern gutgearteter Kinder genießen.

Da saß nun dieses langbeinige, magere Frauenzimmer, das mit seinen sechzehn Jahren so wichtig und altklug die Nase in die Luft hielt, als hätte es nie mit einer Puppe gespielt.

very ashamed for me and she had tears in her eyes when Mr Vollbeck looked at her with rather painful sympathy.

The old donkey made a whole lot of faces each of which was supposed to indicate that he did not see a bright future for me.

"You seem to be of the opinion," he said to me, "that many things do not need to be studied. It appears that your Easter report card was not exactly cause for contentment for your deplorable Mrs Mother. By the way, in my days, it was perfectly acceptable to say Chiology as well."

I was not as much destroyed by these words as Mr Vollbeck assumed, but I was still relieved when Gretchen arrived. She was greeted by her parents with exuberance, very differently than usual, as I had seen from my window. They wanted to show my mother how much joy parents of well-behaved children could have.

There sat this long-legged, scrawny damsel who, with her sixteen years, held her nose up into the air so importantly and precociously as if she had never played with a doll.

»Nun, bist du fertig geworden mit der Scheologie?« fragte Mama Vollbeck und sah mich herausfordernd an, ob ich es vielleicht wagte, in Gegenwart der Tochter den wissenschaftlichen Streit mit der Familie Vollbeck fortzusetzen.

"Now, did you get done with your Chiology?" Mama Vollbeck asked and looked at me challengingly, to see whether I would perhaps dare to continue the scientific argument with family Vollbeck in her presence.

»Nein, ich habe heute abend noch einige Kapitel zu erledigen; die Materie ist sehr anregend«, antwortete Gretchen. Sie sagte das so gleichgültig, als wenn sie Professor darin wäre.

"No, I still have a few chapters to do tonight; the material is very stimulating," answered Gretchen. She said that with such indifference as if she were a professor of the subject.

»Noch einige Kapitel?« wiederholte Frau Rat, und ihr Mann erklärte mit einer von Hohn durchtränkten Stimme:

"Still several chapters?" Mrs Councilor repeated, and her husband explained with a voice brimming with derision:

»Es ist eben doch eine Wissenschaft, die scheinbar gelernt werden muß.«

"It thus must be a science that appears to require studying."

Gretchen nickte nur zustimmend, da sie zwei handgroße Butterbrote im Munde hatte, und es trat eine Pause ein, während welcher meine Mutter halb bewundernd auf das merkwürdige Mädchen und bald kummervoll auf mich blickte.

Gretchen only nodded in agreement, because she had two hand-sized buttered slices of bread in her mouth, and a pause occurred during which my mother looked at the strange girl with half admiration and then with worry at me.

Dies weckte in Frau Vollbeck die Erinnerung an den eigentlichen Zweck unseres Besuches.

This reminded Mrs Vollbeck of the real purpose of our visit.

»Die gute Frau Thoma hat ihren Ludwig mitgebracht, Gretchen; sie meint, er könnte durch dich

"The good Mrs Thoma brought her Ludwig, Gretchen; she thinks he could progress a little in the sciences with your help."

ein bißchen in den Wissenschaften vorwärts kommen.«

»Fräulein Gretchen ist ja in der ganzen Stadt bekannt wegen ihres Eifers«, fiel meine Mutter ein. »Man hört so viel davon rühmen und da dachte ich mir, ob das nicht vielleicht eine Aufmunterung für meinen Ludwig wäre. Er ist nämlich etwas zurück in seinen Leistungen.«

»Ziemlich stark, sagen wir, ziemlich stark, liebe Frau Thoma«, sagte der Rat Vollbeck, indem er mich wieder durchbohrend anblickte.

»Ja, leider etwas stark. Aber mit Hilfe von Fräulein Gretchen, und wenn er selbst seiner Mutter zuliebe sich anstrengt, wird es doch gehen. Er hat es mir fest versprochen, gelt, Ludwig?«

Freilich hatte ich es versprochen, aber niemand hätte mich dazu gebracht, in dieser Gesellschaft meinen schönen Vorsatz zu wiederholen. Ich fühlte besser als meine herzensgute, arglose Mutter, daß sich diese Musterfamilie an meiner Verkommenheit erbaute. Inzwischen hatte die gelehrte Tochter ihre Butterbrote verschlungen und schien geneigt, ihre Meinung abzugeben.

"After all, Miss Gretchen is known for her diligence all over town," my mother interjected. "People hear so much praise and so I thought whether this could not be some encouragement for my Ludwig. He is lagging behind a little in his performance."

"Quite a lot, let's say, quite a lot, dear Mrs Thoma," said Councilor Vollbeck, piercing me with his eyes again.

"Yes, unfortunately a little bit much. But with the help of Miss Gretchen and with some effort that he is going to expend to please his mother, it will be manageable. He has promised me, right, Ludwig?"

Of course I had promised, but nobody could have brought me to repeat my beautiful intention in this company. I could feel better than my goodhearted, naive mother that this ideal of a family found edification in my depravity. In the meantime, the learned daughter had devoured her buttered bread and appeared inclined to give her opinion.

»In welcher Klasse bist du eigentlich?« fragte sie mich.

"What grade are you in anyway?" she asked me.

»In der vierten.«

"In fourth."

»Da habt ihr den Cornelius Nepos, das Leben berühmter Männer«, sagte sie, als hätte ich das erst von ihr erfahren müssen.

"Then you are doing Cornelius Nepos, the life of famous men," she said, as if I had to be told by her.

»Du hast das natürlich alles gelesen, Gretchen?« fragte Frau Vollbeck.

"Of course, you have read this all, Gretchen?" asked Mrs Vollbeck.

22 *Simplicissimus, 1896, #4, p. 5*

»Schon vor drei Jahren. Hie und da nehme ich ihn wieder zur Hand. Erst gestern las ich das Leben des Epaminondas.«

"Three years ago already. Here and there, I pick him up again. Only yesterday, I read the life of Epaminondas."

»Ja, ja, dieser Epaminondas!« sagte der Rat und trommelte auf

"Yes, yes, old Epaminondas!" said the Councilor and drummed

den Tisch. »Er muß ein sehr interessanter Mensch sein.«

»Hast du ihn daheim?« fragte mich meine Mutter, »sprich doch ein bißchen mit Fräulein Gretchen darüber, damit sie sieht, wie weit du bist.«

»Wir haben keinen Epaminondas nicht gelesen«, knurrte ich.

»Dann hattet ihr den Alcibiades, oder so etwas. Cornelius Nepos ist ja sehr leicht. Aber wenn du wirklich in die fünfte Klasse kommst, beginnen die Schwierigkeiten.«

Ich beschloß, ihr dieses »wirklich« einzutränken, und leistete heimlich einen Eid, daß ich sie verhauen wollte bei der ersten Gelegenheit. Vorläufig saß ich grimmig da und redete kein Wort. Es wäre auch nicht möglich gewesen, denn das Frauenzimmer war jetzt im Gang und mußte ablaufen, wie eine Spieluhr.

Sie bewarf meine Mutter mit lateinischen Namen und ließ die arme Frau nicht mehr zu Atem kommen; sie leerte sich ganz aus, und ich glaube, daß nichts mehr in ihr darin war, als sie endlich aufhörte.

Papa und Mama Vollbeck versuchten das Wundermädchen noch einmal aufzuziehen, aber es

on the table. "He must have been a very interesting person."

"Do you have him at home?" my mother asked me, "why don't you talk a little with Miss Gretchen about that, so she sees how far you are."

"We didn't read no Epaminondas," I grumbled.

"Then you had Alcibiades, or something like that. Cornelius Nepos is very easy after all. But if you really going to enter fifth grade, it will begin to get difficult."

I decided to get her for this "really" and secretly swore an oath to beat her up at the first opportunity. For the time being, I grimly sat there and did not say a word. It would not have been possible anyway, because the damsel was in gear and had to rattle on like a music box.

She threw Latin names at my mother and did not allow the poor woman to catch her breath; she poured out all she had inside, and I think she was all emptied by the time she finally stopped.

Papa and Mama Vollbeck attempted to wind up their wonder

girl again, but she had lost interest and quickly walked away to continue studying Chiology.

We stayed back in silence. The happy parents were contemplating the effect all this had had on my mother, and they found it good and acceptable that she was completely smothered. -

In a subdued mood, she took her leave from the Vollbecks and left the garden with me.

Only after we had arrived home, she regained her speech. She tenderly stroked over my head and said: "Poor boy, you will not be able to endure that."

I meant to console her and to promise everything to her, but she only shook her head.

"No, no, Ludwig, that won't work out."

But then it still ended up working out, because soon after my sister got married to Professor Bindinger.

CHAPTER 10: THE WEDDING

Die Vermählung

The Wedding

Ich muß noch die Hochzeit von meiner Schwester mit dem Professor Bindinger erzählen. Das war an einem Dienstag, und ich hatte den ganzen Tag frei. Ich kriegte einen neuen Anzug dazu und mußte schon in aller Früh aufstehen, damit ich rechtzeitig fertig war. Denn es war eine furchtbare Aufregung daheim, und es ging immer Tür auf und Tür zu, und wenn es läutete, schrie meine Mutter: »Was ist denn, Kathi?« Und meine Schwester schrie: »Kathi! Kathi!«, und die Kathi schrie: »Gleich! Gleich! Ich bin schon da«, und dann machte sie auf, und wenn es ein Mann war, der eine Schachtel brachte oder einen Brief, dann kreischten sie alle und warfen ihre Türen zu, denn sie waren noch nicht ganz angezogen.

I still have to tell about the wedding of my sister with Professor Bindinger. It was on a Tuesday, and I had the whole day off. I got a new suit for this and had to get up very early to get ready in time. There was terrible excitement at home, and it constantly went door open, door shut, and when the doorbell rang, my mother yelled: "What is it, Kathi?" And my sister yelled: "Kathi! Kathi!" and Kathi yelled: "Just a minute! Just a minute! I am already here," and then she opened, and if it was a man who brought a package or a letter, then they all screamed and threw their doors shut, because they were not completely dressed yet.

Dann kam ein Diener und sagte, der erste Wagen mit den Kindern ist da, und es ging wieder

Then a servant came and said the first wagon with the children was here, and everything started

los. Meine Mutter rief: »Bist du fertig, Ludwig?«, und Marie schrie: »Aber so mach doch mal!« Und ich war froh, wie ich drunten war.

Im Wagen saß die Tante Frieda mit ihren zwei Töchtern, der Anna und Elis. Sie hatten weiße Kleider an und Locken gebrannt, wie bei einer Firmung.

Die Tante fragte gleich: »Ist Mariechen recht selig? Das kann man sich denken, so einen hübschen Mann, und hätte kein Mensch gedacht, wo er doch dein Professor war!«

Ich wußte schon, daß die alte Katze immer etwas gegen uns hat und, wo sie kann, meiner Mutter einen Hieb gibt. Aber ich habe sie auch schon oft geärgert, und ich sagte jetzt zu der Anna, daß ihre Sommersprossen immer stärker werden. Dann waren wir aber an der Kirche und gingen in die Sakristei, und die Tante mußte es hinunterschlucken und freundlich sein, weil der Herr Pfarrer sie anredete.

Jetzt kam ein Wagen, da war Onkel Franz drin mit Tante Gusti und ihrem Sohn Max, den ich nicht leiden kann. Onkel Franz ist der Reichste in der Familie; er hat eine Buchdruckerei und ist

again. My mother called: "Are you ready, Ludwig?" and Marie yelled: "Come on now!" And I was glad when I was downstairs.

In the wagon sat Aunt Frieda with her two daughters, Anna and Elis. They were wearing white dresses and had curls in their hair as if for a Confirmation.

The Aunt asked immediately: "Is little Marie just in seventh heaven? You can think she is, such a handsome man, and nobody would have thought, he was your Professor after all!"

I already knew that the old cat did not like us and slighted my mother wherever she could. But I had also aggravated her a lot, and now I told Anna that her freckles kept getting more. Then we arrived at the church and went into the sacristy, and the Aunt had to swallow it, because the Reverend started talking to her.

Now a wagon arrived; inside were Uncle Franz with Aunt Gusti and their son Max, whom I could not stand. Uncle Franz is the richest in the family; he owns a book printing shop and is very pious, because he has a Catholic

sehr fromm, weil er eine katholische Zeitung hat. Wenn man zu ihm geht, kriegt man ein Heiligenbild, aber nie kein Geld oder zu essen. Er tut immer so, als ob er lateinisch könnte; er war aber bloß in der deutschen Schule. Die Tante Gusti ist noch frömmer und sagt immer zu meiner Mutter, daß wir zu wenig in die Kirche gehen, und daher kommt das ganze Unglück mit mir.

Wie sie hereinkamen, sind sie zuerst auf den Pfarrer los, und dann hat Tante Gusti die Tante Frieda geküßt, und Tante Frieda sagte: »Du hast ja heute deinen Granatschmuck an. Das können wir freilich nicht.«

Am meisten hat es mich gefreut, daß der Onkel Hans kam mit Tante Anna. Er ist Förster, und ich war schon in der Vakanz bei ihm. Er war lustig mit mir und hat immer gelacht, wenn ich ihm die Tante Frieda vormachte, die verdammte Wildkatze, sagte er. Heute hatte er einen Hemdkragen an und fuhr alle Augenblicke mit der Hand an seinen Hals. Ich glaube, er war verlegen, weil so viele Fremde dastanden, und ging immer in die Ecke.

Die Sakristei wurde immer voller. Von unserem Gymnasium kamen der Mathematikprofessor und der Schreiblehrer. Und dann

newspaper. When you go visit him, you get a picture of a Saint, but never any money or food. He always pretends to know Latin; but he had only gone to a German school. Aunt Gusti is even more pious and always tells my mother that we do not go to church often enough, and that is the reason for all the misfortune with me.

When they came inside, they first tackled the Reverend, and then Aunt Gusti kissed Aunt Frieda, and Aunt Frieda said: "Oh, today you are wearing your garnet jewelry. Of course, we cannot do that."

I was most excited about the arrival of Uncle Hans with Aunt Anna. He is a forester, and I already spent a vacation with him. He had a lot of fun with me and always laughed when I did an impersonation of Aunt Frieda, the damned wild cat, as he said. Today he wore a shirt collar and kept touching his neck with his hand. I think he was shy because so many strangers were standing around, and he kept walking into a corner.

The sacristy continued to fill up. Present from our Gymnasium were the Mathematics Professors and the writing teacher. And

die Verwandten vom Bindinger; zwei Schwestern von ihm und ein Bruder, der Turnlehrer an der Realschule ist und die Brust furchtbar herausstreckte. Mit den Herren fuhren immer junge Mädchen, die ich nicht kannte. Nur eine kannte ich, die Weinberger Rosa, eine gute Freundin von Marie.

Alle hatten Blumensträuße; die hielten sie sich immer vor das Gesicht und kicherten recht dumm, wenn es auch gar nichts zum Lachen gab.

Jetzt kam meine Mutter mit dem Onkel Pepi, der Zollrat ist, und gleich darauf der Bindinger und Marie und der Brautführer. Das war ein pensionierter Hauptmann und ein entfernter Verwandter vom Bindinger. Er hatte eine Uniform an mit Orden, und Tante Frieda sagte zu Tante Gusti: »Na, Gott sei Dank, daß sie einen Offizier aufgegabelt haben.«

Die Tür von der Sakristei wurde aufgemacht, und wir mußten in einem Zug in die Kirche.

Der Bindinger und Marie knieten in der Mitte vor dem Altar, und der Pfarrer kam heraus und hielt eine Rede und fragte sie, ob sie verheiratet sein wollen. Marie sagte ganz leise ja, aber der Bin-

then Bindinger's relatives; two sisters of his and a brother, who is a gym teacher at the vocational school and demonstratively pushed out his chest. The gentlemen were always accompanied by young girls who I did not know. I only knew one of them, Weinberger's Rosa, a good friend of Marie's.

They were all holding flower bouquets; they always held their hand in front of their face and did their stupid giggling, even if there was nothing to laugh at.

Now my mother arrived with Uncle Pepi, who is a Customs Councilor, and immediately after, Bindinger and Marie, and the best man. That was a retired army captain and a remote relative of Bindinger's. He wore a uniform with medals, and Aunt Frieda said to Aunt Gusti: "Ah, thank God that they were able to pick up an officer."

The door of the sacristy was opened, and we had to file into the church.

Bindinger and Marie knelt in the middle in front of the altar, and the Reverend came and gave a speech and asked them whether they wanted to be married. Marie very quietly said yes, but Bindinger said it with a booming

dinger sagte es mit einem furchtbaren Baß. Dann wurde eine Messe gelesen, die dauerte so lange, daß es mir fad wurde.

Ich schaute zum Onkel Hans hinüber, der von einem Bein auf das andere stand und in seinen Hut hinein sah und sich räusperte und am Kopf kratzte.

Dann sah er, daß ich ihn anschaute, und er blinzelte mit den Augen und deutete mit dem Daumen verstohlen auf die Tante Frieda hinüber. Und dann fletschte er mit den Zähnen, wie sie es immer macht. Ich konnte mich nicht mehr halten und mußte lachen. Der Bruder vom Bindinger klopfte mir auf die Schulter und sagte, ich soll mich anständiger betragen, und Tante Gusti stieß Tante Frieda an, daß sie zu mir herübersah, und dann schauten alle zwei ganz verzweifelt an die Decke und schütteln ihre Köpfe.

Endlich war es aus, und wir zogen alle in die Sakristei. Da ging das Gratulieren an; die Herren drückten dem Bindinger die Hand, und die Tanten und die Mädchen küßten alle die Marie.

Und Tante Gusti und Tante Frieda gingen zu meiner Mutter, die daneben stand und weinte, und sagten, es ist ein glücklicher Tag für sie und alle.

bass. Then a mass was read, which took such a long time that I got bored.

I glanced over to Uncle Hans, how kept shifting from one leg to the other, looking into his hat, clearing his throat, and scratching his head.

Then he saw that I was looking at him, and he winked and furtively pointed with his thumb towards Aunt Frieda. And then he bared his teeth the way she is always doing it. I could not contain myself and had to laugh. Bindinger's brother tipped on my shoulder and said I should behave better, and Aunt Gusti nudged Aunt Frieda to look over to me, and then both of them despairingly looked at the ceiling and shook their heads.

Finally, it was over, and we all marched into the sacristy. There, the congratulations began; the gentlemen shook Bindinger's hand, and the Aunts and girls all kissed Marie.

And Aunt Gusti and Aunt Frieda went over to my mother who stood crying by her side, and they said it was a happy day for her and everyone.

Dann umarmten sie auch meine Mutter und küßten sie, und Onkel Hans, der neben mir stand, hielt seinen Hut vor und sagte: »Gib acht, Ludwig, daß sie deine alte Mutter nicht beißen.«

Ich mußte nun auch zum Bindinger hin und gratulieren. Er sagte: »Ich danke dir und hoffe, daß du dich von jetzt ab gründlich bessern wirst.« Marie sagte nichts, aber sie gab mir einen herzhaften Kuß, und meine Mutter strich mir über den Kopf und sagte unter Tränen: »Gelt, Ludwig, das versprichst du mir, von heut ab wirst du ein anderer Mensch.«

Ich hätte beinahe weinen müssen, aber ich tat es nicht, weil Tante Frieda nahe dabei war und ihre grünen Augen auf mich hielt.

Aber ich nahm mir fest vor, meiner lieben Mutter keinen Verdruß mehr zu machen.

Im Gasthaus zum Lamm war das Hochzeitsmahl. Ich saß zwischen Max und der Anna von Tante Frieda. Von meinem Platze aus sah ich Marie und den Bindinger; meine Mutter sah ich nicht, weil sie durch einen großen Blumenstrauß versteckt war. Zuerst gab es eine gute Suppe und dann einen großen Fisch.

Then they also hugged my mother and kissed her, and Uncle Hans, who was standing next to me, held his hat in front of us and said: "Watch out, Ludwig, that they don't bite your old mother."

Now I also had to go over to Bindinger and congratulate him. He said: "I thank you and hope that you will thoroughly better yourself from here on out." Marie said nothing, but she gave me a hearty kiss, and my mother stroked my head and said tearfully: "All right, Ludwig, you will give me that promise, from today on you will be a different person."

I almost had to cry, but I did not, because Aunt Frieda was nearby and had her green eyes fixed on me.

But I took the firm resolve not to cause my dear mother any more trouble.

The wedding feast was in the Lamb's Inn. I sat between Max and Aunt Frieda's Anna. From my place, I saw Marie and Bindinger; I was unable to see my mother, because she was hidden behind a large flower bouquet. First a good soup was served and then a large fish.

23 *Simplicissimus, 1896, #7, p. 4*

Dazu kriegten wir Weißwein, und ich sagte zu Max, er soll probieren, wer es schneller austrinken könnte. Er tat es, aber ich wurde früher fertig, und der Kellner kam und schenkte uns noch mal ein.

With it, we got white wine, and I told Max to see who could down it faster. He tried, but I was done before him, and the waiter came and filled us up again.

Da klopfte Onkel Pepi an sein Glas und hielt eine Rede, daß die Familie ein schönes Fest feiert,

Then Uncle Pepi knocked against his glass and held a speech that the family is having a

133

indem sie ein aufgeblühtes Mädchen aus ihrer Mitte einem wackeren Manne gab und mit ihm ein Band knüpft und die Versicherung hat, daß es zum Guten führt. Und er ließ den Bindinger und Marie hochleben. Ich schrie fest mit und probierte noch einmal mit Max, wer schneller fertig ist.

beautiful celebration by giving a girl in full bloom from its midst to a valiant man with whom they tie a band and be ensured that it will lead to good things. And he let us salute Bindinger and Marie. I enthusiastically screamed along and tried again with Max who could finish first.

24 Simplicissimus, 1896, #7, p. 5

Er verlor wieder und kriegte einen roten Kopf, wie er ausgetrunken hatte. Dann gab es einen Braten mit Salat.

Auf einmal klopfte es wieder, und Onkel Franz stand auf. Er sagte, daß eine Eheschließung sehr erhaben ist, wenn sie noch

He lost again and got a red head when he had emptied his glass. Then we had a roast with salad.

Suddenly there was knocking again, and Uncle Franz got up. He said that marriage is very noble when it is still performed in

in der Kirche gemacht wird und ein Diener Gottes dabei ist.

Wenn aber die Kinder katholisch erzogen werden, ist es ein Verdienst der Eltern.

Darum, sagte er, nach dem jungen Ehepaar muß man an die Alten denken, besonders an die Frau, welche das Mädchen so trefflich erzogen hat; und er ließ meine Mutter leben.

Das freute mich furchtbar, und ich schrie recht laut und ging auch mit meinem Weinglas zu ihr hin. Sie war aufgestanden, und ihr gutes Gesicht war ganz rot, wie sie mit allen anstieß. Sie sagte immer: »Das hätte mein Mann noch erleben müssen«, und Onkel Hans stieß fest mit ihr an und sagte: »Ja, der müßte von Rechts wegen dasitzen, und du bist eine liebe alte Haut.« Dann trank er sein Glas auf einmal aus und schüttelte jedem die Hand, der an ihm vorbeikam, und sagte immer wieder: »Weiß der Teufel, der müßte dasitzen !«

Wir kriegten noch ein Brathuhn und Kuchen und Gefrorenes, und der Kellner ging herum und schenkte Champagner ein. Ich sagte zum Max: »Da ist es viel härter, auf einmal auszutrinken, weil es so beißt.« Er probierte es, und es ging auch, aber ich tat

church in the presence of a servant of the Lord.

But when the children are raised in the Catholic faith, it is to the credit of the parents.

Thus, he said, after the young wedded couple one should consider the elders, especially the woman who raised the girl so splendidly; and he saluted my mother.

I was terribly happy about this and screamed along quite loudly, and I went over to her with my wine glass. She had stood up and her good face was all red as she clinked glasses with everybody. She always said: "If my husband could have seen that," and Uncle Hans clinked her glass hard and said: "Yes, he would rightly sit there, and you are a dear old thing." Then he downed his glass in one, shook the hand of anyone who passed by him, and kept saying: "The devil knows; he should sit there!"

We got another fried chicken and cake and ice cream, and the waiter went around and poured champagne. I said to Max: "That is even more difficult to chug, because it has such a bite." He tried and it actually worked, but I did not participate and sat down by Uncle Hans instead.

136

nicht mit, sondern ich setzte mich zum Onkel Hans hinüber.

Alle waren lustig, besonders die jungen Mädchen lachten recht laut und stießen immer wieder an.

Everybody had a good time; especially the young girls were laughing quite loudly and kept clinking glasses.

Aber Tante Frieda schaute herum und redete eifrig mit Tante Gusti. Ich hörte, wie sie sagte, daß man zu ihrer Zeit nicht so frei gewesen sei.

But Aunt Frieda was looking around and was busy talking to Aunt Gusti. I heard her say that people were not as free as this at her time.

Und Tante Gusti sagte, die Hochzeit ist eigentlich ein bißchen verschwenderisch, aber die Schwägerin hat immer für ihre Kinder zuviel Aufwand gemacht.

And Aunt Gusti said the wedding was really quite frivolous, but her sister-in-law had always expended too much effort on her children.

Da klopfte es wieder, und Onkel Franz stand auf und sagte, daß sein Sohn Max zu Ehren seines verehrten Lehrers, des glücklichen Bräutigams, ein Gedicht vortragen wird.

Then someone knocked again, and Uncle Franz got up and said that his son Max would recite a poem in honor of his respected teacher, the happy groom.

Alles war still, und Max stand auf und probierte anzufangen. Aber er konnte nicht, weil er umfiel und käseweiß war.

Everything went quiet, and Max got up and attempted to begin. But he was unable, because he fell over and was as pale as chalk.

Da gab es ein rechtes Geschrei, und Tante Gusti schrie immer: »Was hat das Kind?«

Then there was a lot of yelling, and Aunt Gusti screamed repeatedly: "What is wrong with the child?"

Die meisten lachten, weil sie sahen, daß es ein Rausch war, und Tante Frieda half mit, daß sie

Most people were laughing, because they saw that it was inebriation, and Aunt Frieda helped bring Max into the next room.

den Max in das Nebenzimmer brachten.

Sie legten ihn auf das Sofa, und es wurde ihm schlecht, und Tante Frieda blieb lange aus, weil sie ihr Kleid putzen mußte. Wie sie hereinkam, sagte sie zu mir, daß ihr Anna schon gesagt hat, daß ich schuld bin, aber niemand paßte auf, weil der Bindinger und Marie fortgingen.

The laid him on the sofa and he got sick, and Aunt Frieda stayed away for a while, because she had to clean her dress. When she came back in, she told me that Anna had already informed her that I was at fault, but nobody paid attention, because Bindinger and Marie were leaving.

Marie weinte auf einmal furchtbar und fiel immer wieder der Mutter um den Hals. Und der Bindinger stand daneben und machte ein Gesicht wie bei einem Begräbnis. Die Mutter sagte zu Marie: »Nun bist du ja glücklich, Kindchen! Nun hast du ja einen braven Mann.«

Marie was suddenly crying terribly and kept embracing mother. And Bindinger stood beside her and made a face fit for a funeral. Mother told Marie: "Now you are so happy, child! Now you have a decent man."

Und zum Bindinger sagte sie: »Du machst sie glücklich, gelt? Das versprichst du mir?«

And she told Bindinger: "You will make her happy, won't you? Will you promise me?"

Der Bindinger sagte: »Ja, ich will es mit Gott versuchen.«

Bindinger said: "Yes, I will try with God."

Dann mußte Marie von den Tanten Abschied nehmen, und unsere Cousine Lottchen, die schon vierzig Jahre alt ist, aber keinen Mann hat, weinte am lautesten.

Then Marie had to say goodbye to the Aunts, and our cousin Lottchen, who already was forty years old but did not have a husband, cried the loudest.

Endlich konnten sie gehen. Der Bindinger ging voran, und Marie trocknete sich die Tränen und

Finally, they could leave. Bindinger walked out first and Marie dried her tears and waved

winkte meiner Mutter unter der Türe noch einmal zu.

»Da geht sie«, sagte meine Mutter ganz still für sich.

Und Lottchen stand neben ihr und sagte: »Ja, wie ein Lamm zur Schlachtbank.«

to my mother again from the doorway.

"There she goes," my mother said quietly to herself.

And Lottchen stood next to her and said: "Yes, like a lamb to the slaughter."

CHAPTER 11: MY FIRST LOVE

Meine erste Liebe

My first love

An den Sonntagen durfte ich immer zu Herrn von Rupp kommen und bei ihm Mittag essen. Er war ein alter Jagdfreund von meinem Papa und hatte schon viele Hirsche bei uns geschossen. Es war sehr schön bei ihm. Er behandelte mich beinahe wie einen Herrn, und wenn das Essen vorbei war, gab er mir immer eine Zigarre und sagte: »Du kannst es schon vertragen. Dein Vater hat auch geraucht wie eine Lokomotive.« Da war ich sehr stolz.

On Sundays, I was allowed to visit Mr von Rupp to eat lunch with him. He had been an old hunting buddy of my Papa's and had shot many bucks with us. It felt very good to be with him. He treated me almost like a gentleman, and when the meal was finished, he always gave me a cigar and said: "You'll be able to handle it, Your father also used to smoke like a locomotive." That made me very proud.

25 Bavarian hunters

Die Frau von Rupp war eine furchtbar noble Dame, und wenn sie redete, machte sie einen spitzigen Mund, damit es hochdeutsch wurde. Sie ermahnte mich immer, daß ich nicht Nägel beißen soll und eine gute Aussprache habe. Dann war noch eine Tochter da. Die war sehr schön und roch so gut. Sie gab nicht acht auf mich, weil ich erst vierzehn Jahre alt war, und redete immer von Tanzen und Konzert und einem gottvollen Sänger. Dazwischen erzählte sie, was in der Kriegsschule passiert war. Das hatte sie von den Fähnrichen gehört, die immer zu Besuch kamen und mit den Säbeln über die Stiege rasselten.

Ich dachte oft, wenn ich nur auch schon ein Offizier wäre, weil ich ihr dann vielleicht gefallen hätte, aber so behandelte sie

Mrs von Rupp was a terribly noble lady, and when she talked, she always pursed her lips to make it sound proper. She always advised me not to bite my nails and to have good pronunciation. Then there was a daughter. She was very beautiful and smelled so good. She did not pay any attention to me, because I was only fourteen years old, and she always talked about dancing and concerts and a blessed singer. In between, she told what had happened in military school. She had learned about that from the cadets who always came to visit and let their sabers rattle across the stairs.

I often wished I was an officer, because then she would possibly like me, but, as is, she treated me like a dumb boy and always

141

mich wie einen dummen Buben und lachte immer dreckig, wenn ich eine Zigarre von ihrem Papa rauchte.

Das ärgerte mich oft, und ich unterdrückte meine Liebe zu ihr und dachte, wenn ich größer bin und als Offizier nach einem Kriege heimkomme, würde sie vielleicht froh sein. Aber dann möchte ich nicht mehr. Sonst war es aber sehr nett bei Herrn von Rupp, und ich freute mich furchtbar auf jeden Sonntag und auf das Essen und auf die Zigarre.

Der Herr von Rupp kannte auch unsern Rektor und sprach öfter mit ihm, daß er mich gern in seiner Familie habe und daß ich schon ein ordentlicher Jägersmann werde, wie mein Vater. Der Rektor muß mich aber nicht gelobt haben, denn Herr von Rupp sagte öfter zu mir: »Weiß der Teufel, was du treibst. Du mußt ein verdammter Holzfuchs sein, daß deine Professoren so auf dich loshacken. Mach es nur nicht zu arg!« Da ist auf einmal etwas passiert.

Das war so. Immer wenn ich um acht Uhr früh in die Klasse ging, kam die Tochter von unserem Hausmeister, weil sie in das Institut mußte.

laughed a dirty laugh when I smoked one of her Papa's cigars.

That often bothered me, and I suppressed my love to her and thought how I would come home an officer from the war when I am bigger, and she would perhaps be delighted. But then I would not want anymore. Otherwise, it was very nice at Mr von Rupp's, and I was always terribly looking forward to each Sunday, to the food, and to the cigars.

Mr von Rupp also knew our principal and often told him that he liked having me in his family, and that I would become a decent huntsman like my father. The principal must not have lauded me much, because Mr von Rupp often said to me: "The devil knows what you always get into. You must be a damned weasel that your professors get on your case like that. Just don't overdo it!" Then, suddenly, something happened.

That went like this. Every morning, when I went to class at eight o'clock, our janitor's daughter came by, because she had to go to the institute.

Sie war sehr hübsch und hatte zwei große Zöpfe mit roten Bändern daran und schon einen Busen. Mein Freund Raithel sagte auch immer, daß sie gute Potenzen habe und ein feiner Backfisch sei.

Zuerst traute ich mich nicht, sie zu grüßen; aber einmal traute ich mich doch, und sie wurde ganz rot. Ich merkte auch, daß sie auf mich wartete, wenn ich später daran war. Sie blieb vor dem Hause stehen und schaute in den Buchbinderladen hinein, bis ich kam. Dann lachte sie freundlich, und ich nahm mir vor, sie anzureden.

Ich brachte es aber nicht fertig vor lauter Herzklopfen; einmal bin ich ganz nahe an sie hingegangen, aber wie ich dort war, räusperte ich mich bloß und grüßte. Ich war ganz heiser geworden und konnte nicht reden.

Der Raithel lachte mich aus und sagte, es sei doch gar nichts dabei, mit einem Backfisch anzubinden. Er könnte jeden Tag drei ansprechen, wenn er möchte, aber sie seien ihm alle zu dumm.

Ich dachte viel darüber nach, und wenn ich von ihr weg war, meinte ich auch, es sei ganz leicht. Sie war doch bloß die Tochter von einem Hausmeister, und ich war schon in der fünften

She was very pretty and wore two large pigtails with red bands and she already had a chest. My friend Raithel always said that she had good potential and was a fine gal.

At first, I did not dare greeting her; but once I did anyway and she turned all red. I also noticed that she waited for me when I was late. She stood in front of her house and peeked into the book store until I arrived. Then she gave me a friendly smile, and I decided to talk to her.

Alas, I did not quite manage with all these heart palpitations; once, I walked up to her very closely, but when I was there, I just cleared my throat and nodded a greeting. I had become all hoarse and was unable to talk.

Raithel laughed at me and said there was nothing to flirting with a gal. He could talk to three girls every day, if he wanted to, but they were all too stupid for him.

I thought about this a lot, and when I was away from her, I also believed it was very easy. After all, she was only the daughter of a janitor, and I was already in fifth grade of Latin school. But

Lateinklasse. Aber wenn ich sie sah, war es ganz merkwürdig und ging nicht. Da kam ich auf eine gute Idee. Ich schrieb einen Brief an sie, daß ich sie liebe, aber daß ich fürchte, sie wäre beleidigt, wenn ich sie anspreche und es ihr gestehe. Und sie sollte ihr Sacktuch in der Hand tragen und an den Mund führen, wenn es ihr recht wäre.

Den Brief steckte ich in meinen Caesar, De bello gallico, und ich wollte ihn hergeben, wenn ich sie in der Frühe wieder sah. Aber das war noch schwerer.

Am ersten Tag probierte ich es gar nicht; dann am nächsten Tag hatte ich den Brief schon in der Hand, aber wie sie kam, steckte ich ihn schnell in die Tasche.

Raithel sagte zu mir, ich solle ihn einfach hergeben und fragen, ob sie ihn verloren habe. Das nahm ich mir fest vor, aber am nächsten Tag war ihre Freundin dabei, und da ging es wieder nicht.

Ich war ganz unglücklich und steckte den Brief wieder in meinen Caesar.

Zur Strafe, weil ich so furchtsam war, gab ich mir das Ehrenwort, daß ich sie jetzt anreden und ihr alles sagen und noch dazu den Brief geben wolle.

when I saw her, it was very strange, and nothing worked. Then I had a good idea. I wrote a letter to her, that I was in love with her, but that I was afraid she would be insulted if I talked to her and told her that. And she should carry her handkerchief and lift it to her mouth if it was alright with her.

I put the letter into my Caesar, *De Bello Gallico*, and I wanted to hand it over when I saw her in the morning. But that turned out to be even more difficult.

On the first day, I did not even try at all; on the next day then, I already held the letter in my hand, but when she came, I quickly put it in my pocket.

Raithel told me I should simply give it to her and ask if she had lost it. I planned to do so, but on the next day, a friend of hers was with her, and then it did not work again.

I was very unhappy and stuck the letter back into my Caesar.

As punishment for being so fearful, I gave myself my word of honor that I would talk to her and tell her everything and moreover give her the letter.

Raithel sagte, ich müsse jetzt, weil ich sonst ein Schuft wäre. Ich sah es ein und war fest entschlossen.

Auf einmal wurde ich aufgerufen und sollte weiterfahren. Weil ich aber an die Marie gedacht hatte, wußte ich nicht einmal das Kapitel, wo wir standen, und da kriegte ich einen brennroten Kopf. Dem Professor fiel das auf, da er immer Verdacht gegen mich hatte, und er ging auf mich zu.

Ich blätterte hastig herum und gab meinem Nachbar einen Tritt. »Wo stehen wir? Herrgottsakrament!« Der dumme Kerl flüsterte so leis, daß ich es nicht verstehen konnte, und der Professor war schon an meinem Platz. Da fiel auf einmal der Brief aus meinem Caesar und lag am Boden. Er war auf Rosenpapier geschrieben und mit einem wohlriechenden Pulver bestreut.

Ich wollte schnell mit dem Fuße darauf treten, aber es ging nicht mehr. Der Professor bückte sich und hob ihn auf.

Zuerst sah er mich an und ließ seine Augen so weit heraushängen, daß man sie mit einer Schere hätte abschneiden können. Dann sah er den Brief an und roch daran, und dann nahm er ihn langsam heraus. Dabei

Raithal said that now I had to do it, because I would be a knave otherwise. I agreed and was very determined.

But suddenly, I was called upon and had to continue. Since I was thinking about Marie, I did not even know which chapter we were on, and I got all red in the face. The Professor noticed that and since he always harbored suspicions against me, he came towards me.

I hastily turned some pages and kicked my neighbor. "Where are we? Goddammit!" The dumb guy whispered so quietly that I was not able to understand, and the Professor was already at my desk. Suddenly, the letter dropped out of my Caesar and lay on the floor. It was written on rose paper and sprinkled with sweet-smelling powder.

I wanted to quickly set my foot on it, but it was too late. The Professor bent over and picked it up.

First he looked at me and let his eyes hang out far enough that one could have cut them off with a scissors. Then he saw the letter and sniffed it; then he slowly pulled it out. In doing so, he looked at me with increasingly

schaute er mich immer durchbohrender an, und man merkte, wie es ihn freute, daß er etwas erwischt hatte.

Er las zuerst laut vor der ganzen Klasse:

»Inniggeliebtes Fräulein! Schon oft wollte ich mich Ihnen nahen, aber ich traute mich nicht, weil ich dachte, es könnte Sie beleidigen.«

Dann kam er an die Stelle vom Sacktuch, und da murmelte er bloß mehr, daß es die andern nicht hören konnten.

Und dann nickte er mit dem Kopfe auf und ab, und dann sagte er ganz langsam:

»Unglücklicher, gehe nach Hause. Du wirst das Weitere hören.«

Ich war so zornig, daß ich meine Bücher an die Wand schmeißen wollte, weil ich ein solcher Esel war. Aber ich dachte, daß mir doch nichts geschehen könnte. Es stand nichts Schlechtes in dem Brief; bloß daß ich verliebt war. Das geht doch den Professor nichts an.

Aber es kam ganz dick.

Am nächsten Tag mußte ich gleich zum Rektor. Der hatte

piercing eyes, and you could tell how elated he was to have caught something.

He started to loudly read in front of the whole class:

"Dearly beloved Miss! Many times, I have been meaning to approach you, but I did not have the courage, because I thought it might insult you."

Then he got to the passage with the handkerchief, and then he only murmured such that the others were unable to hear.

And then he nodded his head up and down, and then he said very slowly:

"You miserable, go home. You will hear about this."

I was so angry that I wanted to throw my books at the wall, because I was such a jackass. But I thought that nothing was going to happen to me. The letter did not contain anything bad; only that I was in love. That was none of the Professor's business, after all.

But then it came down very hard.

The next day, I immediately had to go to the Principal. He had his large book there, into which he

sein großes Buch dabei, wo er alles hineinstenographierte, was ich sagte. Zuerst fragte er mich, an wen der Brief sei. Ich sagte, er sei an gar niemand. Ich hätte es bloß so geschrieben aus Spaß. Da sagte er, das sei eine infame Lüge, und ich wäre nicht bloß schlecht, sondern auch feig.

Da wurde ich zornig und sagte, daß in dem Briefe gar nichts Gemeines darin sei, und es wäre ein braves Mädchen. Da lachte er, daß man seine zwei gelben Stockzähne sah, weil ich mich verraten hatte. Und er fragte immer nach dem Namen. Jetzt war mir alles gleich, und ich sagte, daß kein anständiger Mann den Namen verrät, und ich täte es niemals. Da schaute er mich recht falsch an und schlug sein Buch zu. Dann sagte er: »Du bist eine verdorbene Pflanze in unserem Garten. Wir werden dich ausreißen. Dein Lügen hilft dir gar nichts; ich weiß recht wohl, an wen der Brief ist. Hinaus!«

Ich mußte in die Klasse zurückgehen, und am Nachmittag war Konferenz. Der Rektor und der Religionslehrer wollten mich dimittieren. Das hat mir der Pedell gesagt. Aber die andern halfen mir, und ich bekam acht Stunden Karzer. Das hätte mir gar nichts ausgemacht, wenn nicht das andere gewesen wäre.

wrote everything I said. First, he asked me to whom the letter was addressed. I said it was written to nobody. I had written it just for fun. Then he said that this was an infamous lie, and I was not only bad but also a coward.

That made me angry and I said that the letter did not contain anything mean, and it was a decent girl. Then his two yellow molars were showing when he laughed, because I had given it away. And he kept asking for the name. Now I did not care anymore and I said that no decent man would tell the name, and I would never do so. Then he looked at me sideways and slammed his book shut. Then he said: "You are a rotten plant in our garden. We will rip you out. Your lying won't help you; I know full well to whom the letter is addressed. Out!"

I had to return to the class room, and this afternoon was conference. The Principal and the Religion teacher wanted to expel me. The janitor told me that. But the others helped me out and I just got eight hours detention. That would not have bothered me at all if it had not been for the other.

Ich kriegte einige Tage darauf einen Brief von meiner Mama. Da lag ein Brief von Herrn von Rupp bei, daß es ihm leid täte, aber er könne mich nicht mehr einladen, weil ihm der Rektor mitteilte, daß ich einen dummen Liebesbrief an seine Tochter geschrieben habe. Er mache sich nichts daraus, aber ich hätte sie doch kompromittiert. Und meine Mama schrieb, sie wüßte nicht, was noch aus mir wird.

A few days later, I received a letter from my Mama. In it was a letter from Mr von Rupp, that he was sorry, but he would not be able to invite me anymore, because the Principal had told him that I had written a dumb love letter to his daughter. This he did not care about, but I had brought such a shame on her. And my Mama wrote that she did not know what should become of me.

Ich war ganz außer mir über die Schufterei; zuerst weinte ich, und dann wollte ich den Rektor zur Rede stellen; aber dann überlegte ich es und ging zu Herrn von Rupp.

I was beside myself about this injustice; at first I cried, and then I wanted to confront the Principal; but then I thought about it and went to Mr von Rupp.

Das Mädchen sagte, es sei niemand zu Hause, aber das war nicht wahr, weil ich heraußen die Stimme der Frau von Rupp gehört habe. Ich kam noch einmal, und da war Herr von Rupp da. Ich erzählte ihm alles ganz genau, aber wie ich fertig war, drückte er das linke Auge zu und sagte: »Du bist schon ein verdammter Holzfuchs. Es liegt mir ja gar nichts daran, aber meiner Frau.« Und dann gab er mir eine Zigarre und sagte, ich solle nun ganz ruhig heimgehen.

The maid said nobody was home, but that was not true, because I had heard the voice of Mrs von Rupp outside. I went over again, and then Mr von Rupp was home. I told him everything in all detail, but when I was done, he closed his left eye and said: "You are a damned weasel, all right. I don't really care about this, but my wife does." And then he gave me a cigar and said I should go home in peace.

Er hat mir kein Wort geglaubt und hat mich nicht mehr eingeladen, weil man es nicht für möglich hält, daß ein Rektor lügt.

Man meint immer, der Schüler lügt.

Ich habe mir das Ehrenwort gegeben, daß ich ihn durchhaue, wenn ich auf die Universität komme, den kommunen Schuften.

Ich bin lange nicht mehr lustig gewesen. Und einmal bin ich dem Fräulein von Rupp begegnet. Sie ist mit ein paar Freundinnen gegangen, und da haben sie sich mit den Ellenbogen angestoßen und haben gelacht. Und sie haben sich noch umgedreht und immer wieder gelacht.

Wenn ich auf die Universität komme und Korpsstudent bin, und wenn sie mit mir tanzen wollen, lasse ich die Schneegänse einfach sitzen.

Das ist mir ganz wurscht.

He did not believe a single word and never invited me again, because it is unthinkable that a Principal could be lying.

It was always assumed that the student was lying.

I gave myself my word of honor that I would beat him up once I went to University, the base knave.

I had lost my good spirits for a long while. And then I ran into Miss von Rupp. She was walking around with a few girlfriends, and then they elbowed each other and started laughing. And they even turned around and kept laughing.

When I go University and am a fraternity student, and when they want to dance with me, I will just let them sit there, these snow geese.

That is nothing to me.

CHAPTER 12: THE BABY

Das Baby

In der Ostervakanz sind der Bindinger und die Marie gekommen, weil er jetzt Professor in Regensburg war und nicht mehr hier bei uns.

Sie haben ihr kleines Kind mitgebracht. Das ist jetzt zwei Jahre alt und heißt auch Marie.

Meine Schwester heißt es aber Mimi, und meine Mutter sagt immer Mimili.

Wie es der Bindinger heißt, weiß ich nicht genau. Er sagt oft Mädele, aber meistens, wenn er damit redet, spitzt er sein Maul und sagt: »Duzi, duzi! Du du!«

Es hat einen sehr großen Kopf, und die Nase ist so aufgebogen wie beim Bindinger. Den ganzen Tag hat es den Finger im Mund und schaut einen so dumm an.

Wie sie gekommen sind, ist meine Mutter auf die Bahn, und dann sind sie mit einer Droschke hergefahren.

The Baby

Over the Easter vacation, Bindinger and Marie came to visit, because he was a Professor in Regensburg now and not with us anymore.

They brought their little child along. It is two years old now and also called Marie.

My sister calls it Mimi, however, and my mother always says Mimili.

What Bindinger calls it, I do not know for sure. He often says girlie, but usually, when he talks to it, he purses his trap and says: "Youzee, youzee! You, you!"

It has a very large head, and the nose is bent upwards just like Bindinger's. All day, it keeps its finger in its mouth and looks at you so stupidly.

When they arrived, my mother went to the train station, and then they came here in a horse carriage.

26 Droschke – horse carriage taxi, around 1900

Meine Mutter und die Marie haben das kleine Mädel an der Hand geführt. Der Bindinger ist hinterdrein gegangen.

Über die Stiege hinauf haben sie schon lebhaft miteinander gesprochen, und meine Mutter sagte immer: »Also da seid ihr jetzt, Kinder! Nein, wie das Mimili gewachsen ist! Das hätte ich nicht für möglich gehalten.«

»Ja, gelt, Mama, du findest auch? Alle Leute sagen es. Doktor Steininger, unser Arzt, weißt du, findet es ganz merkwürdig. Nicht wahr, Heini?«

My mother and Marie led the little girl by the hand. Bindinger walked behind them.

On the stairs, they were already chatting lively, and my mother kept saying: "Ah, there you are, children! No, how tall Mimili has gotten! I would not have thought this was possible."

"Yes, really, Mama, you think so too? Everybody says so. Doctor Steininger, our physician, you know, he thinks it is extraordinary. Doesn't he, Heini?"

Dann hörte ich dem Bindinger seine tiefe Stimme, wie er sagte: »Ja, es gedeiht sichtlich, Gott sei Dank!«

Endlich sind sie oben gewesen, und ich bin unter der Tür gestanden.

Meine Schwester gab mir einen Kuß, und der Bindinger schüttelte mir die Hand und sagte: »Ach, da ist ja unser Studiosus! Der Cäsar wird dir wohl einige Schwierigkeiten machen? Gallia est omnis divisa in partes tres, haha!«

Ich glaubte, daß er mich schon examinieren wollte, aber meine Mutter rief: »Ja, Ludwig, du hast ja Mimili noch gar nicht begrüßt und siehst doch dein kleines Nichtchen zum erstenmal! Sieh nur her! Wie lieb und hübsch sie ist!«

Ich fand sie gar nicht hübsch; sie war wie alle kleinen Kinder. Aber ich tat so, als wenn sie mir gefällt, und lachte recht freundlich. Das freute meine gute Mutter, und sie sagte zu Marie: »Siehst du? Ich wußte es gleich, daß ihm Mimili gefallen wird. Sie ist auch zu reizend!«

Im Wohnzimmer war ein Frühstück hergerichtet; unsere Kathi mußte Bratwürste holen, und es gab Märzenbier dazu.

Then I heard Bindinger's deep voice, when he said: "Yes, she's visibly growing, Thank God!"

Finally, they arrived upstairs, and I was standing in the doorway.

My sister gave me a kiss and Bindinger shook my hand and said: "Ah, there he is, our student! Caesar must be posing you some difficulties, right? Gallia est omnis divisa in partes tres, haha!"

I thought he was already trying to test me, but my mother exclaimed: "Oh, Ludwig, you have not even said hello to Mimili yet, and you are meeting your little niece for the first time! Look here! How sweet and pretty she is!"

I did not consider her very pretty; she was like any other little kid. But I pretended to like her and gave a friendly laugh. That made my good mother happy and she said to Marie: "You see? I knew right away that he would like Mimili. She is just too cute!"

Breakfast was laid out in the living room; our Kathi had to fetch bratwursts and we had Märzen beer with it.

Ich freute mich, aber die anderen hatten keine Zeit zum Essen, weil sie immer um das Kind herum waren.

Es mußte seine Hände herzeigen, und wie ihm die Kapuze abgenommen wurde, sah man, daß es blonde Locken hatte, und da schrien sie wieder, als ob es was Besonderes wäre.

Meine Mutter küßte es auf den Kopf, und Marie sagte in einem fort: »Mimi, das ist deine Omama!« Und der Bindinger bückte sich, daß er ganz rot wurde, und sagte: »Du, du! Duzi, duzi!«

Da heulte es auf einmal, und Marie wisperte meiner Mutter ins Ohr, und sie gingen schnell hinaus damit.

Der Bindinger blieb herin, aber er setzte sich nicht zum Essen her, sondern ging auf und ab und machte ein ängstliches Gesicht. Dann rief er zur Tür hinaus: »Marie, es ist doch hoffentlich nichts Ernsteres.«

»Nein, nein!« sagte Marie, »es ist schon vorbei.«

I was excited about that, but the others did not have time to eat, because they were constantly dealing with the child.

It had to show its hands, and when they took its hood off, one could see that it had blond locks, and then they screamed again as if that was something special.

My mother kissed it on the head and Marie kept repeating: "Mimi, this is your grandma!" And Bindinger bent over until he was all red and said: "You, you! Youzee, youzee!"

Suddenly it started wailing, and Marie whispered into my mother's ear, and they quickly took it outside.

Bindinger stayed here, and he did not sit down to eat but paced back and forth and made a concerned face. Then he called through the door: "Marie, I hope it is nothing serious."

"No, no!" Marie said, "it is already over."

27 Simplicissimus, 1896, #9, p. 8

Dann kamen sie wieder herein mit dem Kind, und meine Mutter sagte:

Then they came back in with the child, and my mother said:

»Die lange Bahnfahrt, und dann das Ungewohnte und die Aufregung! Das kommt alles zusammen.«

"The long train ride, and then the unfamiliarity and the excitement! That all comes together."

Ich war froh, wie sie einmal saßen und das Kind auf dem Kanapee ließen, denn die Bratwürste waren schon kalt.

Jetzt fingen wir an zu essen und zu trinken und stießen mit den Gläsern auf fröhliche Ostern an.

Meine Mutter sagte, daß sie schon lange nicht mehr so vergnügt gewesen ist, weil wir alle beisammen sind und Marie so gut aussieht, und das herzige Mimili. Und ich hätte auch ein besseres Zeugnis heimgebracht als sonst.

Ich mußte es dem Bindinger bringen, und er las es vor.

»Der Schüler könnte bei seiner mäßigen Begabung durch größeren Fleiß immerhin Besseres leisten.«

Dann kamen die Noten. Lateinische Sprache III.

»Hm! Hm!« sagte der Bindinger, »das enspricht meinen Erwartungen. Mathematik II-III, griechische Sprache III-IV.«

»Warum bist du hierin so schwach?« fragte er mich.

»Über das Griechische klagt Ludwig oft«, sagte meine Mutter, »es muß sehr schwierig sein.«

Ich wollte, sie hätte mich nicht verteidigt; denn der Bindinger

I was glad when they finally sat down and left the child on the sofa, because the bratwursts were already cold.

Now we started to eat and drink and we clinked our glasses to a Happy Easter.

My mother said that she had not been this jolly in a long time, because we were all together and Marie looks so good as does the lovely Mimili. And I had also brought a better report card home than usual.

I had to bring it to Bindinger, who read it out loud.

"In spite of his lack of talent, the student would be able to perform better with more diligence."

Then came the grades. Latin Language: C.

"Hm! Hm!" Bindinger said, "this meets my expectations. Mathematics: B-C, Greek Language: C-D."

"Why are you so weak here?" he asked me.

"Ludwig often complains about Greek," my mother said, "it must be very difficult."

I wished she had not come to my defense; because Bindinger now

redete jetzt so viel, daß mir ganz schlecht wurde.

talked so much that it made me sick.

Er strich seinen Bart und tat, als ob er in der Schule wäre.

He stroked his beard and acted as if he were in school.

»Wie kann man eine solche Ansicht äußern!« sagte er. »Das ist sehr betrübend, wenn man diesen verkehrten Meinungen immer und immer wieder begegnet. Gerade die griechische Sprache ist wegen ihres Ebenmaßes und der Klarheit der Form hervorragend leicht. Sie ist spielend leicht zu erlernen!«

"How can anyone express such a view!" he said. "That is very saddening, to be confronted with these misguided opinions time and again. The Greek language in particular is exceptionally easy because of its measured rhythm and clarity of form. Learning it is child's play!"

»Warum hast du dann III-IV?« fragte mich meine Mutter. »Du mußt jetzt sagen, wo es fehlt, Ludwig.«

"Then why do you have a C-D?" my mother asked me. "Now you have to say what is amiss, Ludwig."

Ich war froh, daß der Bindinger nicht wartete, was ich sagen werde. Er legte ein Bein über das andere und sah auf die Decke hinauf und redete immer lauter.

I was glad that Bindinger did not wait what I would have to say. He put one leg over the other and looked at the ceiling and kept talking louder.

»Haha!« sagte er, »die griechische Sprache ist schwierig! Ich wollte noch schweigen, wenn ihr den dorischen Dialekt im Auge hättet, da seine härtere Mundart gewisse Schwierigkeiten bietet. Aber der attische, diese glückliche Ausbildung des altjonischen Dialektes! Das ist unerhört! Diese Behauptung zeugt von einem verbissenen Vorurteil!«

"Haha!" he said, "the Greek language difficult! I would keep silent if you had the Dorian dialect in mind, since its harder pronunciation poses certain difficulties. But Attic, the felicitous offspring of the Old Ionic dialect! That is preposterous! This claim is evidence of obstinate prejudice!"

Meine Mutter war ganz unglücklich und sagte immer:

My mother was very unhappy and kept saying:

»Aber ich meinte bloß... aber weil Ludwig...«

"But I was only saying... but because Ludwig..."

Marie half ihr auch und sagte: »Heini, du mußt doch denken, daß Mama es nicht böse meint.«

Marie tried to help her and said: "Heini, you must consider that Mama did not speak with ill will."

Da hörte er auf, und ich dachte, daß er immer noch so dumm ist wie früher.

There he stopped, and I thought that he was still as dumb as before.

»Heini ist furchtbar eifrig in seinem Beruf; sonst ist er so gut; aber da wird er gleich heftig,« sagte Marie, und meine Mutter war gleich wieder lustig.

"Heini is terribly intense in his profession; otherwise he is so good; but there he immediately turns severe," Marie said, and my mother quickly regained her merry mood.

»Das muß sein«, sagte sie, »in seinem Beruf muß man eifrig sein. Und du weißt jetzt, Ludwig, wie leicht das Griechische ist. Ja, was macht denn das kleine Mimili? Das sitzt so brav da und sagt gar nichts !«

"It needs to be like that," she said, "in his job, one has to be intense. And, Ludwig, now you know how easy Greek is. Yes, what is our little Mimili doing? It sits there so nicely and does not say anything!"

Das Mädel schaute meine Mutter an und lachte. Auf einmal machte es seinen Mund auf und sagte: »Gugudada.«

The little girl looked at my mother and laughed. Suddenly it opened its mouth and said: "Googoodahdah."

Es strampelte mit den Beinen und streckte seine Hand dabei aus. Es war doch gar nichts, aber alle taten, als wenn ein Wunder gewesen ist.

It kicked its legs and stretched out its hand. It really was nothing, but everyone acted as if it had been a miracle.

Meine Mutter war ganz weg und rief immer: »Habt ihr gehört! Das Kind! Gugu-dada!«

My mother was beside herself and kept exclaiming: "Did you hear! The child! Googoodahdah!"

»Sie meint, der gute Papa. Gelt, Mimi? Und die liebe Omama!« sagte Marie.

"She means, the good Papa. Right, Mimi? And the dear Gramma!" Marie said.

»Nein, wie das Kind gescheit ist!« sagte meine Mutter. »In dem Alter! Das habe ich noch nicht erlebt. Das liebe Herzchen!«

"Now, how smart the child is!" my mother said. "At that age! I have never seen anything like that. The lovely dear!"

Der Bindinger lachte auch, daß man seine großen Zähne sah. Er bückte sich über den Tisch und stach dem Mädchen mit dem Zeigefinger in den Bauch und sagte: »Wart, du Kleine, duzi, duzi!« Und zu meiner Mutter sagte er: »Sie hat einen lebhaften Geist und beobachtet ihre Umgebung mit sichtlicher Teilnahme. Ich hoffe, daß sie sich in dieser Richtung weiterentwickelt.«

Bindinger was also laughing so one could see his large teeth. He reached over the table and poked the girl into the belly with his index finger and said: "Wait, you little one, youzee, youzee!" And he said to my mother: "She has a lively spirit and observes her surroundings with clear engagement. I hope she continues developing in this direction."

Meine Mutter wollte, daß ich es auch sehe, aber ich war so giftig auf den Bindinger und fragte: »Was hat es denn gesagt?«

My mother wanted me to see it as well, but I was so resentful towards Bindinger and asked: "What did it say?"

»Hast du nicht gehört, wie sie ganz deutlich sagte: Gugudada?«

"Did you not hear her saying very clearly: Googoo-dahdah?"

»Das ist doch gar nichts«, sagte ich.

"But that's nothing," I said.

»Es heißt der gute Papa«, sagte Marie und wurde ganz weinerlich. »Du bist recht abscheulich, Ludwig!«

"It means the good Papa," said Marie, and she got all weepy. "You are real despicable, Ludwig."

»Wie kannst du das nicht verstehen?« sagte meine Mutter und

"How can you not understand that?" my mother said, looking at

schaute mich zornig an. »Das versteht jeder Mensch.«

»Ich kann es gar nicht verstehen«, sagte ich.

»Weil du überhaupt nichts weißt, loser Bube!« schrie Bindinger und machte blitzende Augen, wie in der Schule; »wenn du jemals den Aristoteles kennenlernen wirst, so wirst du begreifen, daß die Sprache unseres Kindes die onomato-poetische, die schallnachahmende Wortbildung ist.«

Er brüllte so laut, daß der Fratz zu weinen anfing. Marie nahm ihn auf den Arm und ging damit auf und ab. Meine Mutter ging daneben und sagte: »Will das Kindchen lustig sein? Will das Kindchen nicht mehr sprechen, gugu-dada?«

Aber der Bindinger lief hinterdrein und sagte: »Nein, es soll nicht sprechen! Es soll hier nicht mehr sprechen! Dieser Bube hat vor nichts Ehrfurcht.«

Ich machte mir aber gar nichts daraus.

me angrily. "Everybody understands that."

"I understand nothing of it," I said.

"Because you do not know anything, you loose boy!" Bindinger exclaimed and made sparky eyes just like in school; "when you ever get to know Aristotle, you will learn that our child's speech is onomatopoetic, creating words to mimic sounds."

He yelled so loud that the little thing started to cry. Marie scooped it up in her arm and walked back and forth. My mother walked beside her and said: "Does the little one want to be funny? Does the little one not want to talk anymore, googoo-dahdah?"

But Bindinger ran after them and said: "No, it should not speak! It should not speak here anymore! This boy does not have respect for anything."

But that did not bother me.

ABOUT THE AUTHOR

Ludwig Thoma was born on January 21st, 1867, in Oberammergau, Germany, as the son of a forester. His father died when Ludwig was seven, so his mother had to raise their seven children on her own. After completing school in 1896, Thoma begins studies in forestry and soon switches to law. He worked as a lawyer until 1899, when he gave up his practice to join the satire weekly *Simplicissimus*. Within a year, he advances to the magazine's chief editor and contributed many pieces sharply critical of state representatives and politics. In 1915, he volunteered as a medic in the war, but had to return home seriously ill. In 1918, he connects with Maidi Liebermann and finds in her the love of his life, although she is and stays married to another man. In the following years, he turns increasingly bitter and anonymously publishes a number of crude, anti-democratic, and anti-Semitic polemics. He expresses the complexity of his character when he writes to his Jewish lover that he has waged war against the "ministers of the old system" and has become used to quarreling. He simply enjoys to "throw big rocks into the duck pond of Berlin." Furthermore, he tells her that "I am not really an anti-Semite, as much as I hate the Eastern Jewish cultural animosity. Besides, I hope to be able to thank the Jewish race for my greatest love," namely Maidi. He died in 1921 from stomach cancer.

ABOUT THE TRANSLATOR

Philipp Strazny was born in Cologne, Germany, exactly - to the day - one hundred years after Thoma. His school years, in contrast, were rather uneventful, without even the slightest threat of ever getting detention. Most rebellious impulses were satisfied vicariously, and - like so many other children - he read Thoma's *Rascal Stories* with glee. After completing his degree in English Studies in 1994, he moved to the United States, where he became a linguist and translator. Today he lives with his wife and children in Manitowoc, WI, works as programmer and localizer for a translation agency during the day, and enjoys translating the books of his youth as a night-time hobby.

For more information, please visit
philippstrazny.blogspot.com.

CPSIA information can be obtained
at www.ICGtesting.com
Printed in the USA
LVHW021731130820
663080LV00021B/2609